About the Author

Cheryl loves nearly everything that is silly and quirky. She also loves Darth Vader, towering mountains, and the natural beauty of Utah where she lives with her family.

The Worldmaker's Assistant

Cheryl Olson

The Worldmaker's Assistant

Olympia Publishers
London

www.olympiapublishers.com
OLYMPIA PAPERBACK EDITION

Copyright © Cheryl Olson 2022

The right of Cheryl Olson to be identified as author of
this work has been asserted in accordance with sections 77 and 78
of the Copyright, Designs and Patents Act 1988.

All Rights Reserved

No reproduction, copy or transmission of this publication
may be made without written permission.
No paragraph of this publication may be reproduced,
copied or transmitted save with the written permission of the
publisher, or in accordance with the provisions
of the Copyright Act 1956 (as amended).

Any person who commits any unauthorised act in relation to
this publication may be liable to criminal
prosecution and civil claims for damage.

A CIP catalogue record for this title is
available from the British Library.

ISBN: 978-1-78830-846-5

This is a work of fiction.
Names, characters, places and incidents originate from the writer's
imagination. Any resemblance to actual persons, living or dead, is
purely coincidental.

First Published in 2022

Olympia Publishers
Tallis House
2 Tallis Street
London
EC4Y 0AB

Printed in Great Britain

Dedication

Jonathan, thank you for always believing in me. Opel, you're my best girl.

1

"Welcome to Good Morning Galaxy! I am your host, Dwilla Cartwiggle, and you are in for a special treat, for with us today is famed worldmaker, Palfrey Dolop!" a purple-haired woman was saying enthusiastically. "Many of you know him as the creator of Funna, the first world consisting entirely of amusement parks, but the latest buzz is all about Palfrey's newest creation, Fooda! It's the first world of its kind and is filled with nothing but delectable restaurants!" The camera zoomed out and Dwilla turned to a golden-haired man seated beside her. "Palfrey, we all know that worldmakers make worlds, but *how* do you do it?"

"Well," Palfrey replied in a smooth voice, "it's something one is born with—the ability to manipulate elements on a massive scale. Of course, one has to go to school to learn how to tap into that ability and fine-tune it."

"An ability you have *definitely* fine-tuned," Dwilla said. "And I must say, I can't wait to go to Fooda and stuff myself full of delicious food! But am I correct in saying that it's been completed for over six months, yet is just now opening to the public?"

"Yes, you are."

"And why is that? That wasn't the case with Funna."

"With Funna, I had nothing to divert my attention, but with Fooda, I had a few personal matters arise," said Palfrey, a shadowed look crossing his face.

Dwilla didn't seem to notice. "And yet, you overcame and succeeded," she said admiringly. "But I can hardly pretend to be surprised as you've done very well with *all* your projects. That's quite an achievement, considering how there's an abundance of uninhabited worlds in our galaxy right now; many worldmakers are hard-pressed to make a living because there's simply *no work* for them to do."

"True," said Palfrey with a sad smile. "I've been incredibly lucky when it's come to opportunity. There are so many gifted worldmakers out there, and any one of them could have done what I have, if not more. I just happened to be in the right places, at the right times."

"You are far too modest," Dwilla said, reaching over and patting him on the arm. "There might be a lot of good worldmakers out there, but to be a *great* worldmaker you have got to have vision, and *you* certainly do!"

"I will agree with you there. I actually…" Palfrey's voice broke off into a chuckle. "I actually went to school with a worldmaker who, whenever he tried to make anything, would turn it straight to mush—not much vision there!"

Palfrey and Dwilla both laughed.

"Well," Dwilla said a moment later, "you have certainly outdone yourself with Fooda. But now that it's finished, what are you planning to do?

"Thank you, Dwilla, but I actually don't have any plans at the moment. Fooda took a lot out of me, creatively speaking, so I'm taking some time off."

"Of course. I *completely* understand; work, no matter what it is, can take so much out of a person. Although, I'm sure I speak on behalf of many, many people when I say I'm disappointed to hear that."

"Yes, well, why don't you enjoy Fooda for now, and then in a few years, we'll see what happens?" Paltry replied, looking slightly annoyed.

Again, Dwilla didn't seem to notice. "You're so right," she said with a smile. Her eyes shifted to the camera. "We have to take a short break, but don't leave, because when we return, we'll be discussing Palfrey's new hit show that's filmed on Fooda, Baking Adventures Fun-Times-For-Everyone-All-The-Time Competition!"

***

V lived and worked in the Deluxe Worldmaker School for Worldmakers, but there was nothing deluxe about its cracked walls, dank rooms, and damp floors. Such conditions were to be expected though, as worldmaking was not a lucrative trade. Just as that show host, Dwilla, had said on the telly, there were too many worlds, which meant not enough work to go around. Palfrey Dolop, worldmaker extraordinaire, was the exception. And yet... despite his fame, money, and charm, he'd sounded so... *unhappy*.

A commercial for a pet-mess vacuum started playing and V returned her attention to washing dishes. Grula, the school's surly cook, often ridiculed her for taking the time to do so, telling her to just throw the dishes on the floor and let the floods do the washing. But, with the assortment of dirty socks and other tidbits that regularly found their way into the kitchen via the floodwater, V couldn't bring herself to do it.

Floods were a common occurrence in the school and happened anywhere from one to seven times a day. This particular day had barely begun and was right on track with a flood of over two-and-a-half feet. The cause was almost always the same: a student trying to use their abilities to take a bath, or fill a cup with water…

Just then, a short, red-faced man swam out of the pantry and into the kitchen where he set up a step stool, climbing to the top of it.

"Hi Jiji," said V. But Jiji didn't respond, which wasn't unusual; as boss of the kitchen, he rarely listened to anyone but himself. For as long as V could remember, he'd been at the school bossing her around and compensating for his shortness by carting around a step stool to stand on.

"Palfrey Dolop, my foot!" he said, clearly having listened to the telly from inside the pantry. "With all his money, you'd think he'd help out more—you know, donate money to worldmaker schools like ours!"

Grula grunted and picked up her tray of freshly made cupcakes. "Donate to the school? Or donate to *you*?" she asked, splashing to the refrigerator and looking a lot like a plump blueberry in her blue hip waders.

"To the school, of course!" Jiji said, swiping a cupcake off the cook's tray as she passed by.

"Yeah, right." Grula scoffed.

"Take that back!" Jiji ordered.

"No!" Grula spat out.

"Yes!"

"No!"

Rolling her eyes, V pulled her dark mane of frizzy curls into a ponytail and stirred together a pot of porridge. But with the telly at her back and nothing else to keep her attention, her thoughts quickly wandered and soon her imagination was spiraling her into the mind realm she so often visited. There, she could see herself on the Dark World, desperately using a human leg bone to scoop the Sapphire of Kirsh out of a boiling pothole of mud...

'...The frenzied cries of Lord Raff's demon henchmen echoed through the air; she was running out of time. Throwing the leg bone aside, she gritted her teeth and reached into the mud, all the skin melting off her arm. Fingers wrapping around the sapphire, she jumped to her feet and ran. In the distance, thick billows of smoke shifted and writhed, making way for something massive and immovable: a cliff. Running to it, she climbed the shelves of rock, the demons close behind her. To fight them off, she reached for her weapon of choice: a crochet hook. But it was too late—a mass of cold, skeletal fingers wrapped around her, tearing through skin and into muscle, scraping across bones. She screamed, but only a low gurgle seeped out, followed by a mouthful of blood frothing over her lips...'

V blinked and the demons disappeared. She blinked again and her surroundings came into focus: the shelf of rock she was clinging to had become the top shelf in the pantry and one of her arms was covered in porridge. Uh-oh, she thought. I've done it again—acted out my imaginations and made another mess! As quickly as she could, she climbed down the shelves and peeked into the kitchen. Porridge was everywhere; she'd flung it onto the walls, the ceiling, Grula's hip waders, and even onto the cupcake in Jiji's hand, like an extra gob of frosting on top.

"*V!*" Jiji sputtered. "*Go!*" He pointed a stubby finger at the door.

Headmaster Baz's office was just around the corner, but to get to it, one had to go through the secretary's office first.

Pushing past a stuffed hippopotamus floating near the doorway, V waded up to a card table. Seated on the other side of it, wearing a black t-shirt that said, 'Don't mess with me, I work for the PPC', was Ophelia, the school's mute secretary.

"I'm here to see Headmaster Baz," said V.

Gazing back at her from behind a pair of glasses festooned in oversized sunflowers, Secretary Ophelia reached out and pushed a button on the table. Bzzz! Bzzz! Bzzz! Bzzz! Bzzz!

The door to Headmaster Baz's office swung open. "*Ophelia*!" A bald man with a scar on the top of his head shouted. "How many times have I told you? That button is *not* a *toy*!"

Secretary Ophelia started filing her nails.

Headmaster Baz threw his hands in the air. "Here I am stuck in a decrepit school with a decrepit secretary and a bunch of decrepit students, and I'm *sick of it!*" With a snap of his fingers, he summoned a mini tsunami from the flood waters and crashed it into Secretary Ophelia's table. Turning to go back inside his office, he spotted V. "And *you*! If you don't give me an aneurysm one of these days from all of your messes, I don't know what will! Unless of course it's *her*...," he pointed at the secretary, "... pushing that button like it's a key on a keyboard!"

A dripping wet Secretary Ophelia reached out and pushed the button again. Bzzz!

Headmaster Baz looked as though he was about to scream, but stomped into his office instead. "Come in, V! And close the door behind you!"

V hurried inside and closed the door before sitting in a chair across from him. Between the two of them was a dinged-up metal desk pockmarked with rust.

"How old are you, V?" he asked.

"Nineteen."

"Exactly. And for nineteen decrepit years I've put up with you." He ran a hand over the scar on his head.

It was a very ugly scar. So ugly, that V couldn't help staring at it; a few years back, a student knocked a turret off the school while summoning wind and Headmaster Baz had chosen that *exact* moment to walk outside. The following few weeks, he'd been on a hefty amount of pain meds and took to singing songs about becoming a space pirate, as well as shouting to anyone who would listen, that his deepest wish was to find Itha's Heart. According to legend, the ancient worldmaker left his heart in the first world he created, a blessing of wisdom and peace to all who lived there…

Headmaster Baz cleared his throat. "What am I going to do with you, V?"

V blinked and met his glare. "I don't know. What *are* you going to do with me?"

"I'd love to send you away—let you be someone else's problem—but I can't. Not when the law clearly states you're the property of this decrepit school. So, you'll just have to stay here, and I'll just have to put up with you. Now get out of my sight before you give me that aneurysm."

V was promptly dismissed to her corner in the basement, which, at that moment, was more of a murky swimming hole. Letting out a huff of air, she teetered on the edge of her bed as it bobbed around in the water and grabbed her slab from underneath her pillow. After writing down some of her thoughts and anonymously submitting them to the local newspaper, she laid back and tried to get some rest, but it wasn't long before she was called to the kitchen; Jiji had made a list of things for her to clean. A very *long* list.

Standing on a ladder, she scrubbed the ceiling and listened

to the telly as a newsman named Tavik gave the planetary midday report,

"...Unrest on the world rises as King Ortho Pip continues to refuse enactment of public peace laws, stating that, 'Rohema has long been a planet fueled by war and savagery. It's who we are, it's what we do.' Meanwhile, the unrest has found its way into the palace as Prince Seff Pip sides with those seeking peace..."

V glanced down and saw a picture of the prince. He had light hair, dark eyebrows, and only one ear.

"...'If the laws are not passed,' he stated earlier this morning on his blog, 'then measures of war will have to be taken. If war is the price that must be paid for peace, we will pay it, but only if absolutely necessary'."

"Tavik," said a second newsman. "Can you expound on what's been happening?"

"Certainly. We're not really sure why, but it's common on Rohema to have one's ears and nose pulled off. This has been an ongoing problem in past years and large numbers of Rohems are fed up with it. A protest demanding laws prohibiting such actions has been scheduled for this afternoon."

"Let's hope they can come to a peaceful resolution," said the second newsman. "Thank you, Tavik. Now, for our daily stock report: Hidium shares have gone up, while shares in both Sole and Dirsta have dropped..."

V glanced at the telly again, this time seeing the picture of a woman standing in front of a T-shaped glass building. Red hair, pouty lips, impeccable makeup... There was no mistaking who she was: Ursa Dazzle-Razzle, spokeswoman for Threka Industries, the first company to be created and owned by a robot. But that wasn't all—she was also the girlfriend of Xander Verin, the school's only non-worldmaker instructor. Ever since his arrival a few weeks before, the subject of Scientific Theory of Combining Elements had become very popular and there was never any shortage of girls to swoon over his beautifully shaped cheekbones and feathery dark hair. But, whenever Ursa came to visit, the swooning morphed into sobbing, and hail storms were abundant.

"...Threka Industries, although new to the board, has had an incredible increase in shareholders over the past few weeks and today stocks have gone up over—"

The stock report cut out and the words, 'Emergency news report,' scrolled across the telly.

V stopped scrubbing.

"Hey," Jiji called from the pantry. "What did they say about the Threka stocks?"

"Get out here and see for yourself," Grula grunted.

The live footage of a planet V didn't recognize, started playing. Hovering next to the planet was a black, crescent-shaped ship.

"With all of Hulse's satellites incapacitated..." a woman was saying, "... this feed is coming from the nearby planet, Arca. Caught barely a minute ago on the security satellites, it was immediately transmitted to the PPC, or Planetary Peace Council. A specialized fleet has been sent to contend with the ship, but—"

Suddenly, a bright light flashed. When it died down, V felt as though someone had kicked her in the ribs, forcing every particle of air from her lungs.

Hulse had exploded.

2

Wide-eyed, V watched the smoke around Hulse clear; at least two-thirds of the planet's overall mass had been obliterated. Dust and ash and rock floated around what was left of its rocky core. The black ship was nowhere to be seen.

"There goes another one. Eight down, probably more to go," Grula grunted.

A click sounded and the channel changed to the cook's favorite show, Baking Adventures Fun-Times-For-Everyone-All-The-Time Competition. A preview for the upcoming contest showed sixteen people baking inside a pastel-rainbow teepee, all of whom were making cream puffs that would be donated as building material for huts on remote planets.

"The PPC's behind this!" Jiji suddenly exclaimed. "They've gotten too overloaded with all the new planets so they're doing away with the oldest ones!"

"You and your conspiracy theories," grumped Grula.

"They're not theories!" Jiji retorted. "They're *facts*!"

Grula snorted.

The rest of the day went by in a blur. The floods had finally receded, but V's arms and hands ached from all the scrubbing and scraping Jiji had assigned her to do. And her head hurt from thinking about how, if she'd been on Hulse, she would've found a way to infiltrate the black ship, rewiring the weapon system so it would implode as she sped away in an escape pod. Only, she never made it onto the escape pod. No matter how many times she imagined it, it was always out of reach and every time, she died a horrible death. Rubbing her forehead, she grabbed one of Grula's few remaining cupcakes out of the refrigerator and took a bite.

"Drat, now my very expensive shoe has gotten stuck in a bucket of flour, and I can't see to get it out..."

Bewildered, V looked around the kitchen to see who had spoken, but as far as she could tell, she was alone.

"It's going to cost a lot of money to get it cleaned..."

The voice seemed to be coming from inside the pantry. Cupcake in hand, she went to investigate.

"I wonder if that short little man with the step stool knows how to clean shoes...?"

She opened the pantry door. Squinting into the darkness, she saw Xander Verin, or, *Instructor* Verin, as he was called in the school, sitting on a box, his lower left leg and foot stuck inside a bucket of flour. *"Instructor Verin?"* She was more than a little surprised. In all her years at the school, she'd never happened upon an instructor in the pantry. Sneaking into the refrigerator, yes. But not the *pantry*—everything in there had to be baked or cooked and none of the instructors knew how to do either of those things. "What are you doing in here? It's the middle of the night."

Alarm flashed across Instructor Verin's face. "Quiet!" he whispered. Clambering to his feet, he clunked over to her and clamped a hand over her mouth. He also bumped her arm, causing the cupcake she was holding to fly into the air. Up, up, up it went before falling down, down, down and landing on his nose with a *splat!* "Oh no! My perfect nose!" he cried. Grabbing the cupcake, he tossed it over his shoulder, into the dark pantry. He then used both hands to carefully scrape frosting off his face.

Horrified, V waited for him to yell at her, but instead, he began licking his fingers, seemingly delighted by the flavor of the frosting.

"Yum!" he exclaimed. "This is *so* good!" He looked at V. "Perhaps you could go get another one…? Before…?" His voice tapered off and the delighted expression on his face was replaced by one of the upmost seriousness. "Nope," he said, taking hold of her elbow and whisking her into the pantry. "There's no time. You'll just have to stay here with me until they get here. If you haven't noticed by now," he said, closing the door most of the way, leaving only a small crack to see through, "I'm a spy and I can't let you blow my cover."

"Wait…" dizzy from the sudden movement, V grabbed his arm to steady herself, "…*what*?"

"Did I say all of that aloud?" he mused. "What I meant to say was *spider*. Pantries are *great* places to find spiders, and I'm going to catch one for my *book* cover."

V scrunched up her nose. "You like spiders and you're making a *book cover* out of them?"

"Yes, but it's not something I really talk about." Instructor Verin peeked into the kitchen through the cracked-open door. A few moments of silence passed. "Where are they?" A faint glow lit the pantry as he checked the watch on his wrist.

"Who? The spiders?"

"Yes."

Creeeeeeeak.

Skeptical, V squeezed past him and looked for herself. No spiders were in sight. There were, however, three men entering the kitchen through the creaky kitchen door. Two of them were at least seven feet tall and were wearing long, dark robes with hoods that obscured their faces. The third man was much shorter in comparison and had a very ugly scar on the top of his head. "Headmaster Baz," she whispered.

Letting out a phony sounding chuckle, Instructor Verin tugged her away from the door. "I wonder what *he's* doing here…" Another chuckle. "What a *coincidence*…." He nodded to the back door that was used for bringing in supplies. "You should go now, only go out that way, so he doesn't see you."

"Then how am I supposed to get back inside the school? All the doors and windows are locked."

"I don't know," said Instructor Verin with a shrug. "Maybe you could get a ladder or something?"

"A ladder?" How would that help?"

"Not sure, but best be on your way." He stepped to the side and tripped over the bucket on his foot, crashing face-first to the floor. "Help!" he softly cried. "Get it off!"

V quickly reached down and pulled the bucket off.

Just as quickly, he jumped to his feet and began climbing a row of shelves on the wall, the same row of shelves V had climbed earlier that day.

"Hey!" she hissed. "*What* are you doing?"

"They've heard us! Hide!"

"No, they haven't!" She peeked into the kitchen just to be sure and saw Headmaster Baz and the two men rummaging through the fridge. Suddenly, a "Humph!" sounded behind her. It was followed by an "Ouch!" and a snap. A loud thud was next and then several thumps and cling-clang-snap-cracks that were most certainly shattering glass jars. Whipping around, she saw Instructor Verin groaning on the floor beside two broken shelves.

"What was that?" asked a deep voice in the kitchen.

"Go find out," said Headmaster Baz.

Uh oh, thought V. She ran to the back door and opened it before returning to Instructor Verin, dragging him behind a stack of boxes.

Seconds later, the pantry door swung open, light spilling into the room.

"What do you see?" Headmaster Baz called out.

"Not much," the deep voice replied. "Just food scattered across the floor... broken bottles... a cupcake... The back door is open."

"Man-eating raccoons," growled the headmaster. "Decrepit creatures, always breaking in, biting off arms and legs." Pause. "I *have* got to get out of this decrepit school." Another pause. "Close the door. I'll talk to that decrepit V tomorrow and remind her to check the locks at night. Otherwise, she'll be sleeping in the gardening shed."

V cringed. That was outside... with the raccoons!

"Who's V?" another deep voice asked. "And is V an expert allium cepa grower? All the gardeners have quit, so I'm in need of a good allium cepa grower."

"You and your allium cepas," snapped Headmaster Baz. "Couldn't you be bothered to eat something else?"

"No." The deep voice sounded hurt. "I've told you before that I *have* to eat them—it's a condition I was born with: *alliumcepatitis*."

"Sorry. I forgot," said Headmaster Baz, not sounding sorry at all. "But V is not an expert allium cepa grower, so focus on the task at hand."

Meanwhile, inside the pantry, heavy feet crunched over broken glass. The back door clicked shut. The feet crunched across glass again and the door to the kitchen shut, leaving V and Instructor Verin in darkness.

"I didn't think that would work," Instructor Verin said, letting out a low groan.

V felt him move around, his elbow jabbing her in the arm.

"I thought we were done for," he continued.

"We almost were," V replied, wincing and rubbing her arm. "I mean, I think we almost were—I'm actually not sure what Headmaster Baz would have done had he caught us in here." An image of the gardening shed popped into her head.

"I am," said Instructor Verin. "He would have had our ears and noses pulled off—those men weren't messing around."

"Ears and noses pulled off?" V's eyes widened. "Why would he do that?"

"I can't tell you what I don't know, but hopefully, I'll know more by the end of their very important conversation." The space behind the boxes illuminated with the light from his watch. "Now, how do I get back to the door without crashing into or breaking anything else?"

It dawned on V then, what was really going on. "You made up the whole thing about spiders, didn't you? I really *did* hear you say you were a spy—you're in here to spy on Headmaster Baz. But *why*?"

"Uh…" Instructor Verin's face went blank. "I can't tell you. If I did, I would have to tickle your feet and paint your toenails."

V raised an eyebrow. "Is that a good thing or a bad thing?"

"Bad. Very bad—I hate other people's feet. So, can you show me to the door?"

"If it's really that important," said V, who was starting to wonder if the stunning instructor was really just a dunce-head.

"It is."

"Okay." She let out a bewildered breath. "I'll be right back." Crawling out from behind the stack of boxes, she used the small shaft of light coming from beneath the door to mentally plot the safest and quietest way to it. "This way," she said.

Minutes later, the two of them inched up to the door. Coming from the other side of it were muffled blips of, "Goo gah rooh rah" and "uble wubble fubble bubble…"

"What are they saying?" V asked.

"Don't know," replied Instructor Verin. "It sounds like they're speaking gibberish. Or it's maybe Rohemish. The two are very similar."

The gibberish or Rohemish abruptly stopped. Following were some shuffling sounds that turned into scuffling sounds.

"Give that to me!" demanded the deep voice of the person who had come into the pantry.

"No!" the other deep voice said. "It's *my* turn! You got it last time!"

"You clot! I'm older, so I *always* get it first!" The first voice bellowed.

"Maybe so, but I'm a p—"

"Hey!" It was Headmaster Baz. "I'm the headmaster, give it to *me*!"

More scuffling followed and then came the sound of the telly turning on,

"…As you can see, the contestants are each adding their own twist to a fruit pie. Bunsof is adding olives and paprika to his eggplant and apple pie, Stully is adding chili and lime to her strawberry-rum pie, Sissily is adding chocolate and caramel to her cherry pie, and Claybell is adding ginger and mint to her carrot-blackberry-banana pie…"

"Are they watching the Baking Adventures Fun-Times-For-Everyone-All-The-Time Competition?" V whispered incredulously.

"I think so," Instructor Verin whispered back. "Great show, isn't it?"

"Sure, but definitely not worth spying for. I mean, is this the *real* reason you're in here? To listen to them watching the telly?"

"Don't be silly—of course that's not why I'm here. *But,* seeing as they *are* watching it, we might as well enjoy it too, right?"

"I guess…" V listened as Hawali's garlic-ginger-pickle-mango pie was badly underdone and burnt on the edges, and Gursna's apple-broccoli-sugar pie was perfect. But in the end, it was Bunsof's eggplant and apple pie which won and Sissily, with her chocolate and caramel-cherry pie, who got sent home.

After the show ended, the telly clicked off. A whole chorus of 'uggle buggles' followed and then the sound of the refrigerator opening and closing. The clang of plates and silverware came next, then more gibberish or Rohemish. And eventually, the sound of footsteps, the lights clicking out, and the kitchen door opening and closing as the three men left the room.

3

Exhausted, V crawled into bed, only to be awakened minutes later by the school's rusty messenger bot tromping into the basement and announcing in a loud, crackly voice that she was needed in the kitchen, *immediately*. Wondering what it would be like to someday go an entire night without any sort of disruption, she put on some clothes and shuffled upstairs.

"What took you so long?" Jiji practically yelled when she stepped into the kitchen. Standing on his step stool, he was eating a red cupcake that matched his red face. Behind him, scattered across the countertops and table, were the dirty plates and empty containers of food left by the headmaster and his friends.

"I was asleep."

"You don't get paid to sleep! You get paid to clean!"

"Actually, I don't get paid at all. And I was going to clean it, I just wanted to get some sleep first."

Jiji looked ready to explode. "After making a mess like *this*?"

"I didn't make this mess," said V.

"Is that so?" Jiji retorted accusingly. "If you didn't do it, then who did?"

"Uh…" V's eyes flickered to the pantry; from what she could tell, he hadn't seen that mess yet, but what was she supposed to say about the other mess? Blaming the headmaster wouldn't go over well...

Ghosts, she quickly decided upon. Yes, that was it. "It was the ghosts," she announced.

The blood drained from Jiji's face. "*Ghosts?*"

"Yeah, I hear them rattling the silverware at night."

Hopping off his step stool and tucking it under his arm, Jiji ran out of the kitchen.

Yawning, V went to the cleaning closet to get some rags.

One of the kitchen doors creaked open. "Hello?" Someone said.

V's stomach clenched; it was Instructor Verin. But why was he back? To spy on someone else?

"Hello?" he said again. "Is anyone here?"

No! she thought. *Go* away! I don't want any more messes! Ducking behind a row of aprons, she watched him head straight into the pantry.

Snap.

He came out a few seconds later and skittered out of the kitchen.

Wondering what he'd been up to, and what that strange snaping sound had been, she brushed the aprons aside and hurried to the pantry.

It was spotless.

She rubbed her eyes; she was seeing things—it was still a mess; she was just too tired to see it.

Nope. It was spic and span.

***

A few hours later, V was back in the kitchen. She was beyond tired, but that didn't stop her from thinking about Instructor

Verin and the pantry. As a direct result, there were no wild, mess-making escapes into her imagination, and she was finished with her chores by mid-afternoon.

A news report was playing and a woman was informing the galaxy that Rohema would indeed be preparing for civil war and that the PPC would not be getting involved unless alliances were formed with other planets.

V finished eating her sandwich and scanned the kitchen; Grula was beatboxing the theme song to the Baking Adventures Fun-Times-For-Everyone-All-The-Time Competition, and Jiji was fast asleep on his step stool. Sucking in a deep breath and wondering if she wasn't taking too much of a risk, she waded into the hallway and was soon standing outside Instructor Verin's flooded classroom. Sitting at his desk, he was reading a yellow book and brushing his hair. He was also rubbing a few fingers over the bridge of his very straight nose. Softly clearing her throat, V stepped into the room.

Instructor Verin looked up and the brush slipped from his hand, falling into the water. His other hand dropped from his nose as he fumbled with the book, shoving it inside the top drawer of his desk. "V!" he said, hastily folding his arms. "What a pleasant surprise! Is there something I can assist you with?"

"Well…," V couldn't help admiring how nice his hair looked, but then mentally kicked herself; she wasn't there to ooze and gush all over him—there were more than enough girls willing to do that—*she* was there to get *answers*. "Yes." She squared her shoulders and smoothed her shirt, which looked more like a tattered old tent than an article of clothing. "I was hiding in the cleaning closet when you went into the pan—"

Instructor Verin sprang out of his chair and splashed over to her, one of his hands clamping over her mouth. "Not so loud," he whispered, looking at the door.

She looked at the door too, and seeing no one there, batted his hand away. "Stop doing that!" she hissed. "You could just ask me to be quiet."

Instructor Verin smiled sheepishly. "Sorry. It's a habit of mine."

For a moment, V didn't say anything. "Did you just say that putting your hand over people's mouths is a *habit*?"

"Yes, but you're the only one who seems to mind it." His brow furrowed.

After a few seconds of staring at him like he was crazy, she said, "Look, I didn't mean to interrupt your reading and hair brushing, I just really want to know how you cleaned the pantry so quickly. It's been eating away at me all day—I can't stop thinking about it."

Instructor Verin cocked his head to the side and smiled again. "Aren't you going to thank me?"

"No. Why would I?"

"Because it's something people do when they are appreciative of something someone else has done for them. In your case, I cleaned the pantry so you didn't have to."

"Oh… " V slowly began. "So because you made the mess and then cleaned it up, you want a thanks?"

"Yes."

She didn't feel that his actions warranted any thanks at all, but in the interest of getting answers said, "Thank you, I guess."

Instructor Verin bowed, both arms flapping out at his

sides. "Not the best thank you I've ever gotten, but it will do. Now, off with you—I have work to do." He turned to go to his desk, but V grabbed his arm.

"No—I'm not leaving until you tell me how you did it."

"Mmm. After everything that went wrong last night, you really expect me to tell you?"

"Went wrong? Everything that went wrong was *your* fault—gigantic mess included."

"No. I beg to differ, not about the mess part, but about everything else—if you'd just stayed out of the pantry everything would've been *fine*."

"If *I'd* stayed out of the pantry? Out of the two of us, I'm the one who had the most reason for being there, seeing as I *work* there."

"That's hardly fair," Instructor Verin retorted. "Because as of last night, I was working there, *too*."

Just then, a sharp clap of thunder came from the hallway. It was followed by the sound of several small somethings pelting the walls and floodwater. More thunder ensued. A few moments later, a shapely, red-haired woman splashed through the open classroom door. Held above her head like a makeshift umbrella, was an embroidered black bag topped with a pile of hailstones. The woman was Ursa Dazzle-Razzle.

"What is it with hailstorms popping out of nowhere whenever I visit?" she exclaimed, looking at Instructor Verin. "I swear…" Her voice tapered off the moment she noticed V, her full, red lips turning down in visible disgust. "What's this?" she demanded, her piercing copper eyes shooting to the instructor. "Have you taken to instructing rodents now? And what exactly is your plan for this one? To have it dancing around you with a single snap of your fingers?"

V's mouth fell open; she'd never heard Ursa speak in person before, but now that she had, it was easy to see the woman was a downright witch and deserved every hailstone she got.

"Will you please excuse us, V?" asked Instructor Verin.

V didn't have to be asked twice.

Later that day, after the school had dried out for the fifth time, she was midway through her snack break when a knock sounded on the door of the kitchen cleaning closet. It was the messenger bot.

"Headmaster Baz wishes to see you," it said.

Stuffing a last bite of apple into her mouth, she headed to his office. Sitting at Secretary Ophelia's card table was a bouquet of fuchsia daisies wearing yellow glasses and a black t-shirt with, 'PPC=BFF' printed across the front. V squinted at the flowers, eventually making out a face beneath all the petals. "Headmaster Baz sent for me," she said.

The bouquet of daisies pressed the red button on the table. Bzzz! Pause. Bzzz! Bzzz! Bzzz! Bzzz!

The door to the headmaster's office opened and a visibly irritated Headmaster Baz stepped out. Raising a hand in the air, he snapped his fingers and a mini tornado appeared beside Secretary Ophelia's table. "Come in, V," he said, retreating to his desk.

Hurrying after him, V shut the door. On the other side of it, the tornado was making a terrible ruckus: crashing, smashing, howling…

"Now," said Headmaster Baz, appearing quite pleased with himself. "I have called you here because raccoons—" A very loud knock interrupted him, and his eyes shot to the door. Following another snap of his fingers, the howling, crashing, and smashing stopped. "Come in," he said, looking irritated again.

The door opened and someone entered the office. A someone who was wearing a long, dark robe with a hood that shadowed his face; a someone who was so tall and broad that he seemed to absorb every bit of space in the room. But this someone also had one of Secretary Ophelia's fake plants stuck to the top of his head, as well as an assortment of fake leaves, flowers, and papers clinging to his robe. V quickly realized that the someone was one of the hooded men from the night before, and he looked so ridiculous that a snort of laughter escaped her.

Headmaster Baz cleared his throat. "Unless you'd like your own tornado visit, V, I would apologize to my friend for being so rude."

"Right." She coughed and quickly collected herself before looking at the hooded man. "I'm sorry," she said, extending a hand to him to show she truly *was* sorry.

The man silently stepped forward, clasping her hand in his—a hand which only had four fingers. Where the fifth finger should have been was a scarred stump. After a brusque handshake, he returned to his spot beside the door.

V turned to Headmaster Baz only to find him staring at her so intensely that she worried he would send a tornado visit anyway. But then, his focus shifted to the hooded man,

"You must excuse her—she's never met anyone from your planet so you cannot expect her to know of your customs." He refocused on V. "As I was saying a moment ago, raccoons broke into the pantry last night. If you don't want to live in the gardening shed, make sure you're locking the doors before you go to bed."

"Okay."

"Good." Headmaster Baz put on his reading spectacles.

"Is that it?" she asked.

"Yes. Unless there's something else you'd like to discuss? Just be warned that if you say 'yes,' I will plough down this entire decrepit school with a hurricane."

"No." V quickly shook her head. She was used to the headmaster's antics and threats, but so far that day, they'd been more ominous than usual.

"Then get out of here before you give me an aneurysm." Headmaster Baz scowled at her before turning to the hooded man. "You're early," he said, picking up a piece of paper.

Fleetingly, V caught a glimpse of it: the word 'Threka' was written in bold, black letters in the upper left corner. And right below that, was a five with an enormous amount of zeros trailing behind it.

4

On the way out of Headmaster Baz's office, V was startled to see the tornado-ravaged state of Secretary Ophelia's office. Along with the clutter of papers, chairs, flowers, fake plants, and a stuffed hippopotamus teetering halfway out the window, her table and chair were stuck upside-down in the ceiling. The bouquet of fuchsia daisies that was actually Secretary Ophelia, was sitting in the upside-down chair with a phone to her ear. When her eyes met V's, she quickly hung up, smirked, and pushed the red button. Bzzz! Bzzz! Bzzz!

Before another disaster could blow through, V sprinted out of the office and down to her corner in the basement where she found a note lying on her pillow. It read,

Dearest V,

What I told you last night is true—I *am* a spy. I've been sent to this school to investigate Headmaster Baz in connection to Threka. They're an engineering firm known for the manufacture of the pet-mess vacuum. Only, they're making a lot more money than can be accounted for by their product, which leads me to believe that the pet-mess vacuum is just a front for their *real* industry. I've tried to meet with the bot in charge, but it's quite elusive. And there's been mention of something called a *zaret*, but no one seems to know what it is. There are also rumors that they've been manufacturing illegal weapons, but I have nothing to prove that. Thus, Headmaster Baz is my only lead, but other than becoming filthy rich from investing into the company, he's squeaky clean. Which brings me to the point of this note: I need you to sneak into his office and find something suspicious that links him to Threka. Tonight is the quarterly faculty meeting which will provide the perfect amount of time for you to do so. It will also deflect suspicion away from me since I'll be in the meeting with him.

You're my only help,
Instructor Verin

P.S. When the meeting is over, I'll meet you in the pantry, seeing as you work there.

A few hours later, V was hurrying down the hallway, her mind racing with a list of unfortunate things Headmaster Baz might do to her if he ever found out what she was doing. At the top of that list was living in the gardening shed. Next was a tornado visit. But there were other things, too: being locked in the dusty, old storage room for the rest of her life, her bedroom being moved into the moldy bathroom on the far side of the basement… And yet, her decision hadn't been a hard one to make: if she helped Instructor Verin, then perhaps he would help her leave the school.

Upon reaching the headmaster's office, she went straight to his desk. Her plan was to find the paper she'd seen him holding earlier, the one that had 'Threka' printed on it. But it wasn't in any of the drawers. Not sure where else to look, she went to the only shelf in the room and started leafing through the books. Several minutes passed before she came to one with a faded, blue cover. Opening it, she was both surprised and pleased to find two pieces of paper tucked inside. The first one was the Threka paper. The second one was an application to be in the Baking Adventures Fun-Times-For-Everyone-All-The-Time Competition.

"How odd," she muttered. "I didn't know Headmaster Baz liked to bake."

She quickly made copies of the papers and went to put them back when a word on one of the books' pages caught her attention: *zaret*. Setting the papers on the desk, she tried to read more, but the book was written in another language. Disappointed, she returned it to the shelf and noiselessly left the room.

A short while later, she was in the kitchen making a burrito. Suddenly, her head jerked up as she remembered the papers—they were still on Headmaster Baz's desk! Rushing back to his office, she put them away and was turning out the light to leave when footsteps echoed in the hallway. Seconds later, the door to Secretary Ophelia's office opened.

"Are you sure it will work?" a deep voice asked.

Hurriedly, V ran to the window, drawing the tattered, floor-length curtain over her.

"Yes. So long as we all do our parts correctly," Headmaster Baz replied. The light to his office flipped on. "Decrepit secretary; I told her to close my door when she left."

"Maybe that tornado addled her brain," another deep voice said.

"Addled or not, she should still follow a simple non-decrepit order," the headmaster griped.

Meanwhile, V was struggling to stay the swaying curtain with her fingertips and peeped through one of its many holes to see if anyone had noticed. Headmaster Baz was standing by the shelf with one of his tall, hooded friends. They were looking through the book she'd found the papers in, earlier. The headmaster's other tall, hooded friend was facing the curtain. She shrank back as he walked towards her, stopped right in front her, smelling of, what was it? Cinnamon? Cinnamon rolls and macaroons? Wrinkling her nose and resisting the urge to sneeze, she waited for him to tear the curtain aside... but he *didn't*.

"Praise the stars that everything is finally coming together," Headmaster Baz was saying. "I don't know how I've survived for so long in this decrepit hole, watching my potential slowly flush down the toilet. Someone of my skill should be doing things of importance, not leading the next generation of useless, jobless, decrepit brats."

"You *are* doing something of importance," said the hooded man beside him.

"I know—it's just hard being patient."

Eyes watering, V bit her lip and closed her eyes; the scent of macaroons and cinnamon was so strong... *too* strong. Unable to move without bumping into the man on the other side of the curtain, a little 'achoo!' escaped her.

"What was that decrepit sound?" asked Headmaster Baz.

Oh no! V thought, bracing herself for the worst.

"I think it was a sneeze," said the man beside the headmaster. "A very girly sneeze."

"It was," the man on the other side of the curtain said abruptly. "It's the dust."

V's terror turned to shock; why was he covering for her? He *knew* she was there—she'd just sneezed on him through the curtain.

"I didn't realize you had such a weak constitution," said Headmaster Baz. "Or such girly sneezes."

"Me neither," said the man beside him.

"Your office is dusty," retorted the man on the other side of the curtain.

"He speaks the truth," said the man beside the headmaster. "It is quite dusty in here."

"Nor did I realize that both of you were such decrepit pansies," said Headmaster Baz. "But I suppose your feebleness when it comes to dust is our sign to leave—there's not much time before the deadline."

Cracking open an eye, V peeped through the hole again and saw the headmaster hand one of the papers from the book to the man beside him.

"Make sure he takes the fall for this, and I'll take care of the rest," Headmaster Baz said, before he and the man left the room.

The man on the other side of the curtain followed close behind, turning off the light and closing the door with a hand that only had four fingers.

V waited a few minutes before sneaking out from behind the curtain and hastily grabbing the faded, blue book. Tiptoeing back to the window, she used a shaft of moonlight to illuminate the remaining paper tucked inside its pages: the Threka paper. The application for the Baking Adventures Fun-Times-For-Everyone-All-The-Time Competition was gone.

5

Back in the kitchen, V was completely exhausted and completely puzzled; why hadn't the hooded man with four fingers told Headmaster Baz she was hiding in his office? It had to be only a matter of time before he did so. He was, after all, friends with the headmaster, not her. And after she'd laughed at him earlier that day, who knew what he'd do to her? Was an apologetic handshake enough to deter him from hunting her down and possibly tearing off her nose and ears? To distract herself from that befuddling, terrifying thought, she finished making her burrito, ate it, and let her mind escape to the Dark World…

'…Having retrieved the Sapphire from the Bleak Tomb of Bernerd—whoever Bernerd was, a relative of Lord Raff, perhaps?—she dashed through the Burnt Forest, heading straight for the spaceship that would fly her to Crystlin, the planet where everything was wonderful and good. But those blasted demons were right behind her. How did they always catch up to her so quickly? She felt around her belt for something to throw at them, but having lost her trusty crochet hook, deadly scissors, and ghastly knitting needles, she was completely defenseless. Well, not *completely*. She picked up rocks and threw them over her shoulder. As well as handfuls of dirt. And fish heads…'

Fish heads? V blinked. She was standing beside the open

freezer, holding a fish head in each hand. "What...?" Turning to see what horrors she'd cast upon the rest of the kitchen, she saw several bags of powdered sugar strewn across the room and dozens of apples splattered on the walls.

Upset with herself for making another mess, she quickly got to cleaning and turned on the telly for background noise. An episode of Baking Adventures Fun-Times-For-Everyone-All-The-Time Competition was just wrapping up. In it, the competitors had been required to make fully functioning spaceship engines out of fondant, and not only did they have to *look* good, but they absolutely had to *taste* good. After that was the late-night news,

"Prince Seff Pip of Rohema, and his bodyguard, Kesh Yib, have just been named competitors in that baking show with the really, really, *really* long name. Only moments ago, the prince told reporters that his participation on the beloved show is a last desperate attempt to convince his father that peace and civility are what their people need.

"We have to take a short commercial break, but when we return, we'll have more on this story, as well as some updates on the planet-destroying ship that is now being called the *Planet Destroyer*."

A catchy jingle about getting a pet-mess vacuum followed, and V turned off the telly. The kitchen was clean, and it was getting late. Her eyes went to the pantry; so far, there'd been no sign of Instructor Verin.

Suddenly, the pantry door opened and out walked a bouquet of fuchsia daisies.

"Secretary Ophelia?"

The bouquet of fuchsia daisies nodded and gave her a thumbs up before leaving the kitchen.

Instructor Verin walked out of the pantry next, his left foot stuck inside another bucket of flour and a newspaper in one of his hands. In his other hand was a comb. "Oh, hi V. I was just about to come looking for you."

"Instructor Verin? I don't understand—how long have you been in there?"

"A while. You were busy throwing apples and we didn't want to disturb you."

V's face turned bright red; up until that point, Jiji and Grula were the only ones who'd seen her making messes. "Why was Secretary Ophelia here?"

Instructor Verin ran the comb through his hair. "She and I were discussing some important business."

"About school?"

"Of course not—she's a spy, too."

"Really?"

"Yes. It was actually her idea to have you sneak into the headmaster's office—I got a phone call from her earlier."

"Oh…" V remembered seeing Secretary Ophelia on the phone, but had assumed she was just cleaning it; as a mute, it would be quite difficult to carry on a conversation with the person on the other end. Although… being a spy, she must have figured out a way to do so…

"Were you able to find anything?" Instructor Verin asked.

"What?" V blinked a few times before realizing what he'd asked her. "Oh, yeah." She slipped the copied papers out of one of her pockets and handed them to him. "These are just copies. One is some sort of financial document. The other is an application for the Baking Adventures Fun-Times-For-Everyone-All-The-Time Competition."

Instructor Verin arched one of his dark, straight eyebrows. "I didn't know Headmaster Baz liked to bake."

"Yeah, me neither," said V, thinking then that there were

probably *a lot* of things about him they didn't know. "Oh, and the book I found them in said something about a *zaret*, but it was written in another language."

"How very curious." Instructor Verin ran the comb through his hair again. "Is there anything else?"

"Yes, actually." She quickly told him about her going back to the office to put the papers away and then hiding behind the curtain when the headmaster returned with his friends. "Headmaster Baz said something about a deadline and that if they all did their parts it would work, and that it was important."

"What would work? What was important?"

"I don't know, but they took the application. And Headmaster Baz said, 'Make sure he takes the fall for this, and I'll take care of the rest,' whatever that means." She refrained from mentioning how the man on the other side of the curtain had discovered her, but hadn't done anything about it; how could she expect someone else to believe her when she could hardly believe it herself?

A smile tugged at the corners of Instructor Verin's lips. "Excellent work, V. I must admit, you've far exceeded my expectations."

Cheeks growing warm with pleasure, she bit her lip. She wanted to ask him right then and there to help her leave the school, but decided to let it wait until morning when she wasn't so tired or covered in powdered sugar and mushed apples.

"Goodnight, then." Instructor Verin turned and clunked towards the kitchen door.

"Wait!" called V. "The flour bucket on your....!" But before the word *foot* could form in her mouth, he tripped over the bucket and toppled to the floor. She hurried over to him and pulled the bucket off. "Are you okay?" she asked, helping him to his feet.

"Yes, thanks." Instructor Verin brushed a lock of feathery hair from his face. "You should go to bed, you look tired. And read this while you're at it." He handed her his newspaper and left the kitchen.

She waited until the door shut behind him to look at it. Her stomach lurched; it was opened to the newest 'Perpetually Unending Story' article. Was that just a coincidence? Or did Instructor Verin know her secret? She decided the best course of action was to throw the newspaper in the trash, but then, curiosity got the better of her. Pulling out a chair from the kitchen table, she sat down to read it,

'Gasping for breath at having just climbed out of one of the Dark World's many cavernous pits, the Sock-Mender, Lagatha, ran through the woods. The demon henchmen were close on her heels, but she was almost to the rendezvous point where the spaceship would pick her up and take her to Crystalin.

Suddenly, she tripped over a bulging tree root and the beloved Sapphire of Kirsh flew out of her hand. Screaming in horror, she watched a demon swallow it whole. Leaping to her feet—one of which was bent sideways with the bone sticking out of it—she grabbed a spare knitting needle from her belt and hobbled to the demon, gouging the Sapphire out of its throat.

Howling with rage, the other demons flung themselves at her, their claws and teeth tearing into her skin.

Her blood spraying everywhere, Lagatha held the Sapphire high above her head. "Lord Raff will never get this!" she cried. "He will never…!'

That was the end of the article.

6

That night, when V crawled into bed, she found another note lying on her pillow:

V,

I need you to get the book—the one you told me about earlier? I could do it myself, but seeing as you know which one it is, I'll just let you do it.
Instructor Verin

The thought of sneaking back into Headmaster Baz's office made V queasy. And yet, she had dreams that needed to be actualized. Half sighing, half groaning, she slipped the note beneath her pillow. Next thing she knew, a bucket of cold water splashed onto her face. But it wasn't a bucket of water at all—her room was flooded again, almost to the ceiling.

Rolling off her mattress, she swam up to the main level of the school and opened the nearest door, tumbling out onto the lawn. Other than the water, the rest of the building seemed to be in order... except for one room in the science wing. Squinting, she saw it was completely flooded, but not in the usual way; half the water was rushing up to the ceiling while the other half was rushing down to the floor.

Realizing that the Elemental Water instructor was holding another midnight practice session—one that clearly wasn't going so well—she found some rocks and threw them at the window. Instantly, the glass shattered, torrents of water and a handful of students rushing up into the night sky. She let out a sigh of relief. But then, the rest of the windows burst making the school look like a fountain of water in which half the waterspouts were going up and the other half were going down.

In a matter of minutes, the grounds had become a scene of complete chaos; waves crashing, furniture smashing, shards of glass falling from the sky, bleeding students and instructors struggling to stay afloat...

Scrambling up a nearby tree, V narrowly avoided a fast-moving current carrying Jiji on his step stool. Grula and her hip waders whipped by a second later. Bringing up the rear was Secretary Ophelia, who appeared to have made a lifejacket out of flowers.

Suddenly, the waterspouts shut off and several screams sounded as those who'd been airborne rained down on the flooded grounds. At the same time, Headmaster Baz drifted out the front doors of the school on a raft. Before long, the water dissipated, but not without leaving everyone soggy, and the lawn littered with stray bits of glass, furniture, papers, clothes, and books.

"Books!" V exclaimed, clamping a hand over her mouth. A few dripping students looked up at her before scrambling to pick up all the books around them. But she didn't care—not about *their* books. She scanned the area for Headmaster Baz and found him speaking to some instructors. Seeing that he was more than preoccupied, she jumped down from the tree and ran to the other side of the school, scrambling into his office through the broken window.

7

The following morning, V awoke to the messenger bot shouting down the stairs in a crackly, booming voice, "Headmaster Baz says to clean this decrepit school, *immediately*!"

The school was a mess, much worse than she was used to, which was really saying something. Groaning, and trying not to think about things like naps and fluffy pillows, she rolled out of bed and got to work. Starting at her corner in the basement, which had accumulated everything from a cafeteria table to a student stuck behind the washing machines, she quickly worked her way upstairs and by lunch time, had finished the entire main floor. By late-afternoon, she'd worked herself into the science wing. By early evening, she was just entering Instructor Verin's classroom.

Ursa Dazzle-Razzle was sitting in the instructor's comfortable looking swivel chair, the heels of her fancy red rain boots propped up on his desk. Her copper eyes narrowed at V. "Finally! Now this glob-awful mess can be taken care of!" She waved a few glossy, red-nailed fingers through the air. "Shoo, shoo, get to work, cleaning-girl!"

Instructor Verin was standing at the far end of his desk, his very straight nose buried in the same yellow book V had seen him reading the day before. "Now Ursa," he chirped. "You could at least say please." Lowering the book, he winked at V.

That didn't go unnoticed by Ursa.

"I *never* say please to rodents," she said scornfully. "And I'm starting to wonder if your taste has soured—you actually seem to *like* having them around."

"Now, Ursa…"

Any other day, V would have let Ursa's words roll off her shoulders, but this particular day she had no patience for snobby, short-sighted remarks and snapped, "Clean it yourself, Ursa! You lazy, fancy, big-haired buffalo!" Tightly gripping the brooms, mops, and buckets of rags in her arms, she unsteadily spun on her heel and lumbered out of the classroom. Footsteps echoed behind her in the hallway and moments later, Instructor Verin jogged up alongside her.

"V," he said, in a serious tone of voice, "you should know that speaking to others that way doesn't suit you."

"Doesn't suit *me*?" V almost laughed. "That woman doesn't suit *you*—she's absolutely awful!"

"Mmm." Instructor Verin rubbed a few fingers over his nose and then took hold of V's arm, pulling her into an adjacent closet full of spiderwebs and empty mop buckets. "Maybe so," he said, closing the door and turning on the light. "But she does buy me expensive shoes."

"Shoes or not, you can't seriously be okay with her speaking to you that way, can you?"

A peculiar expression crossed his face and he plucked a comb out of his pocket, running it through his hair. "Well, that's enough about me—you obviously wanted to speak with me about something, otherwise you never would've lured me into this closet."

"Lured you into this closet? *What* are you talking about?"

By now, V was used to the instructor's eccentricities, but it didn't make them any less confusing, or at that moment, irritating. "*You* brought *me* in here."

"Is that so?" He put the comb away. "In that case, I should let you go. As fun as this is, we can't always be chatting away the days in closets." He turned to open the door when V remembered something.

"Wait!" she said.

"Now, V, I already told you that as fun as this is—"

"I got the book."

"You *did*?"

V nodded.

"Excellent!" Instructor Verin smiled. "How about you bring it to my room later tonight. Shall we say, ten? Ursa will be gone by then and I'll just be going over lesson plans."

"Yeah. Sure."

"Oh, and just so you know," he whispered, as they stepped out of the closet. "I had to calm Ursa down after what you said, so I explained to her that you're suffering from *cupcakitosis*, a disease in which you have to eat cupcakes regularly throughout the day or else you lose all control over what you're saying. And as of right now, you're severely cupcake deprived, so I suggest you go eat some."

"Cupa-whata?" Due to her armful of cleaning supplies, V couldn't see her feet and tripped over a loose floorboard. She quickly regained her balance, but a bucket of rags lurched out of her arms and hit the instructor right in the nose.

Everything that followed seemed to happen in slow motion: Instructor Verin let out a shrill wail and covered his face, tottering back inside the closet where he got a mop bucket stuck on each foot. Wailing again, he tottered out, spun in a few wobbly circles and then ran off crying about how his perfect nose had been ruined.

***

At ten-o-clock sharp, V stepped into the classroom. Instructor Verin was sitting at his desk. The spots beneath both of his eyes, and his nose, were a dark shade of purple.

"Hello, V," he said. "Good to see you."

Apprehension fluttered through V; all afternoon she'd rehearsed her apology to him, but now that he was right in front of her, she wasn't sure how to begin. "That's from the bucket, isn't it?" she said, eyeing his bruised face.

"The bucket?" Instructor Verin reached up to touch his nose, but then stopped. "Oh yes, the bucket. I do believe so."

"I'm really sorry. I didn't mean for that to happen; it just flew out of my arms and—"

"It's okay," he cut in. "Sometimes buckets hit you in the face, or get stuck on your feet, that's just how life is. But let's not dwell on that—I believe you brought me something?"

"Yeah." She pulled the faded, blue book out from under her shirt and handed it to him. "This is it." As he looked through the pages, she again contemplated asking him to help her leave the school, but after what she'd done to his nose, would he even consider it? Perhaps it was best to wait until he got better... Swallowing the lump in her throat, she turned to leave.

"Don't go yet," said Instructor Verin. "I have something for you."

"You do?" V didn't hide her surprise.

"Yes." He handed her a piece of paper.

"What's this?"

"An apology—for what happened earlier."

"An apology?" Raising an eyebrow, V gingerly took the paper and read what it said:

Dearest V (is that really your name, or is it short for something else?),

I want you to know that I'm truthfully sorry for having a girlfriend that isn't very nice sometimes (okay, a lot of times) and that makes you say mean things that don't suit you, so that you run away, and I have to chase you down and talk to you inside a closet, after which you trip, and a bucket whacks my beautiful, perfect nose.

I'm also sorry for all the times I haven't been, or may not be, forthright with you. But I am a spy, and I have to do my job.

Sincerely,

Xan

P.S. You can't call me Xan. Even though I prefer it to Instructor Verin, it's only proper that you continue to call me Instructor Verin.

V looked up and Instructor Verin gave her an imploring look.

"Well, what do you think?" he asked.

"What do I think?" she repeated.

Instructor Verin nodded.

"Oh.... Um…" She thought for a moment; she didn't want to cause any hurt feelings. "It was… nice."

"I thought so, too. And your name?"

"My name?"

"Yes. Is it short for something else?"

"Oh. No, I don't think so. No one's ever told me it is."

"Well then, question answered." Instructor Verin flashed an anxious smile. "Now, if you'll sign the apology all will be well."

"Sign it? Why would I do that?"

"To give me peace of mind; the next time Ursa's around and says something and you say something back, yada, yada, yada, and a bucket whacks me in the nose, I can look at it and know that everything's okay."

"It will help you know that everything's okay? That doesn't make any sense."

"Yes, I know. But having this signed apology from me to you will just help me remember that."

"Okay…" It still didn't make sense to V, but she set the apology on the desk. "Where do I sign?"

Instructor Verin tapped a spot near the bottom of the paper. "Right here will be fine." He handed her a pen.

"That's a little low, don't you think?"

"No, on second thought, it's actually not low enough." He tapped the very bottom edge of the paper.

V was skeptical but didn't object. Uncapping the pen, she bent over to sign. At the same time, Instructor Verin switched the apology with another piece of paper. But it was too late, she'd already signed it. Her eyes shot to his face. "What was that about? What did you just have me sign?"

"The apology, of course." He hurriedly took the papers and shoved them into the top drawer of his desk.

"No, it was a different piece of paper. You switched it out—I *saw* you do it."

"No, you didn't, it was just that overactive imagination of yours." He rubbed a few fingers over his nose, smudging the dark purple color.

"No, it wasn…" V's eyes focused on the flesh showing through the purple smudge. "Is that… *makeup*?" she gasped. An unexpected pang of hurt ricocheted through her chest. "You just wanted me to think your nose was bruised?" Hurt quickly morphed into anger. "Show me that paper you made me sign, right now!"

"Shhh!" Instructor Verin said, glancing at the door. "You'll attract attention!"

As much as V hated agreeing with him right then, she knew he was right—the last thing she wanted to do was attract attention. "Give me that paper you made me sign," she said quietly.

"No, I can't do that," he replied, just as quietly.

"Yes, you can."

"Nope, not gonna happen." He snatched the two papers out of his desk, grabbed the faded, blue book, and wildly ran out of the room, arms flapping through the air.

V stared after him, mouth slightly ajar until she came to her senses. Hands clenching into fists and gritting her teeth, she started to leave as well, but then noticed something on the desk: the yellow book. Despite her better judgement, she grabbed it and ran out of the room in much the same manner as Instructor Verin had—minus the wildly flapping arms, that is.

8

V collapsed onto her bed. Why had Instructor Verin put on that makeup? And *what* had he made her sign? With an angry huff, she opened his yellow book and flipped through it. The pages themselves were blank but taped to them were clippings of the 'Perpetually Unending Story' articles. Stopping on one that had a big red question mark and a very suspicious looking V drawn at the bottom of it, her eyes skimmed across the words:

'Lagatha huddled beneath an overhanging boulder. She was cold. Her muscles ached from having just swum across the Black Lake. Her skin felt like it was on fire from where the acid eels had latched onto her, pulling her underwater. If not for that random zap of lightning electrifying them, and her inborn resistance to incredibly high volts of electricity, she'd be dead.

She coughed, drops of blood splattering onto her hand; it was a miracle she'd made it this far. It was a miracle the demons hadn't torn her into bits, eating her for their dinner. It was a miracle that falling off that random cliff in the middle of nowhere hadn't broken every bone in her body. It was a miracle that a cloud had been waiting midway down the cliff to catch her. It was a miracle that the smoky, sulfuric air, and the acid eels, and the bottomless depths of the Black Lake hadn't gotten her. It was a miracle that every time she thought she was going to die, she didn't. But miracles were what she needed, because leaving the Dark World without the Sapphire of Kirsh meant death. Not only for her, but for the entire

Universe. Such power should not have been placed in such a small, tangible object. The Galactic Wizards realized their mistake now, but it was too late: aside from her, all the Sock Menders, the bravest warriors in the galaxy, were dead.

A high-pitched shriek vibrated through the thick, pungent air and the ground shuddered; the demons had found her, but there was nowhere to go. Nowhere except for... down. Lagatha peered into a jagged opening in the ground; if she was ever going to survive this, she had to go down there. And if she was ever going to get the Sapphire, she had to go down there. But that was also where the demons were born, and surely, they would overcome her down there...'

A heaviness settled inside V's chest; reading the articles, and knowing that others were reading them too, should have made her happy, but it didn't. It was just a reminder to her that she'd be stuck in a shabby, rundown, worldmaker school for the rest of her life.

Sighing, she started to close the book when a white piece of paper slipped out from between the pages. Printed on it, in swirly black ink, were the words, Certified Worldmaker. Right below that, was a name: Ooblick Oofser.

Ooblick Oofster? she wondered. Who's that? And why does Instructor Verin have his worldmaker certificate? Grabbing her slab, she typed in the name and waited. After a long couple of seconds, a profile appeared,

'Ooblick Oofser: worldmaker.
Origin: Elcrata solar system.
Planet: Ton.
Age: 27.
Attended: Ton Worldmaker University (TWU).

Status: single.
Accomplishments: none.
Whereabouts: probably dead.'

V did a double take—probably dead? What happened? She scrolled down the screen to learn more, but there was nothing. She scrolled back up and reviewed the information; Ton was the name of Ooblick's home planet, but why did it sound so familiar? She clicked on the name and an article popped up:

'Ton Destroyed. The First Planet to be Ravaged by the Dreaded Planet Destroying Ship.'

Feeling a little sick, she backed out of the screen and clicked on Ooblick's name, instantly recoiling when a picture of a young man appeared. Dark, rat's nest of hair, long bulbous nose, pasty skin... She shut off the slab and stuck it under her pillow.

The next day, she toted the book and certificate around with her, hoping to return them to Instructor Verin without his noticing. But every time she went by his classroom, he was either teaching or sitting at his desk, brushing his hair. Giving up on returning the items any time soon, she set them on her nightstand and trudged up to the kitchen to do her afternoon chores. Grula was watching another episode of Baking Adventures Fun-Times-For-Everyone-All-The-Time Competition, and Jiji was snoring in the pantry.

Washing the walls, scrubbing the oven... It wasn't long before V's mind went on a visit to the Dark World where her escape transport had been destroyed, preventing her from leaving...

'...On a rickety raft constructed from bundles of bones,

she steered through the violent waves of lava. Up ahead, loomed the Mount of Nor, a dark shadow against the even darker night.

Suddenly, a great serpent surfaced in the lava, its black head and glistening snout twice the size of the raft. Opening its foul-smelling mouth, it dove at her, but she was too quick, jumping out of the way and using a very large pair of scissors to cut clean through its neck. The head dropped into the lava. The wriggling, severed neck sank down beside it. But then, just as the head was about to disappear beneath the flaming, red waves, a slithery, pink tongue shot out and tightly wrapped around her, pulling her in...'

Another death-filled ending.

V frowned and inspected her work; the inside of the oven had been scrubbed clean to a shine. There were, however, some slash marks that appeared to be from a pair of scissors in her hands—a pair of scissors she didn't remember grabbing. She backed out of the oven to see if Grula or Jiji had noticed anything—some loud scratching noises, perhaps? But the two of them seemed completely oblivious to her presence; Jiji and his step stool were heading to the toilet and Grula was molding a lump of dough into a scorpion. Relieved, V got to work scrubbing hotplates, but halfway through the scrubbing, and another reverie of escaping the Dark World with the Sapphire, a picture on the telly caught her attention: it was Ursa. The baking show had ended, and the daily news report was on,

"Threka stocks have reached a record high. An incredible feat for an engineering firm that was once so small it fit inside of this tiny shop."

Another picture appeared. It showed a large cardboard box that had a door and some windows cut out of it. Right beside the box was a tiny bot that stood roughly two feet high: the head of Threka Industries.

The picture of Ursa returned,

"Ursa Dazzle-Razzle, Spokeswoman for Threka Industries, has been chosen to speak at the annual Forever Young and Good-looking Entrepreneur For Life Conference next month, where she will not only divulge some of the secrets to Threka's success, but also the secrets of her youthful appearance. Most people believe she is in her early twenties, but she is actually well into her nineties..."

"Ugh!" V exclaimed. "Instructor Verin, what are you *thinking*?" Disgusted, she slammed her scrub brush down on a hotplate and resumed scrubbing. Money, she reasoned. It had to be the money. And it didn't hurt that Ursa *did* look pretty amazing, even for a twenty-year-old.

"Ahem."

She glanced up to see Grula eyeballing her, a how-dare-you-speak-of-an-instructor-so-rudely-sort of expression on her face. V took a deep breath and tried to smile. "What I meant to say, is that Instructor Verin is very lucky to have such a well-developed, geriatric girlfriend."

Grula's expression softened and she nodded. "Just don't go forgetting your place," she grunted, returning her full attention to the scorpion-dough.

V finished the hotplates and had just moved on to the microwave, when a bot tromped into the kitchen, but it wasn't the school's bot. This bot was bigger, bulkier, shinier, and most definitely newer.

"V, you must come with me," it said in a clear, mechanical voice.

Surprised, V set down her scrub brush. "Okay." She

followed the bot all the way to Headmaster Baz's office. Heart thumping, several questions raced through her mind: where had the shiney, new bot come from? Why had the headmaster sent for her? Did he know about her taking his book? Had the man with four fingers finally told him that she'd been hiding in his office?

"Take a seat," Headmaster Baz said. Wearing his reading spectacles, he was shuffling through a stack of papers. "You're not here to be reprimanded, this is merely a checkup to see how you're doing."

V's forehead wrinkled. "It is?" In all her life, Headmaster Baz had never cared to 'see how she was doing'.

"Yes. How are you feeling? Any sicknesses? Sudden desires to shove dozens of cupcakes into your mouth at once, or to start yelling horrible things?"

"What? No. Of course not. I feel fine."

"Anxieties I should be aware of?"

"No." V was getting worried; was something wrong with her? Something she wasn't aware of, but other people were? The only out-of-the-ordinary thing she'd done recently was take Headmaster Baz's book, and Instructor Verin's book. Clearly, she was turning into a book burglar, but what did that have to do with cupcakes and yelling? Had Headmaster Baz been speaking with Instructor Verin?

"All right then," said Headmaster Baz. "I just had to ask." He gestured to the bot. "Go ahead and scan her."

"What's this about?" V asked when the bot was done. But the bot didn't respond. She looked at Headmaster Baz. He was shuffling through the stack of papers again.

"Don't tell me you've forgotten already?" he said, glancing up at her. "Perhaps I should change your assessment to unfit?"

"No." V quickly shook her head.

"I didn't think so." Standing up, Headmaster Baz handed the stack of papers to the bot.

"We are grateful for your oversight," the bot said. Papers in hand, it turned and tromped out of the room.

V watched it leave and then looked at the headmaster. She wanted to ask him what in the worlds was going on, and what oversight had been made, but didn't want to sour his surprisingly caring mood.

"You're excused, V," Headmaster Baz said. "Don't make me regret my decision."

"I won't," she said, all the while wondering what his decision had been.

"Good. Now go before I change my mind."

9

Woosh, woosh, thump, thump, thump... Woosh, woosh, thump, thump, thump...

Down in V's corner of the basement, the washing machines clattered loudly as she tried to sort her thoughts of what had just happened. But what *had* just happened? Headmaster Baz hadn't mentioned anything about his book or about her hiding in his office. She wasn't in trouble. So why *was* she summoned? Why was there a strange, shiney bot? And *why* had the headmaster suddenly seemed to sort-of care about her? Wriggling inside of her was the feeling that Instructor Verin was somehow behind it; why else would Headmaster Baz have mentioned cupcakes?

She flopped back-first onto her bed, something jabbing between her shoulder-blades. "Ouch!" She leapt to her feet and turned to see what it was. Laid out neatly, right below her pillow, was a metal spatula, a pair of pink shoes, and a pink dress with cupcakes printed on it.

"What in the worlds...?"

Carefully setting the spatula and shoes aside, she held up the dress for a better look. What was it doing in the basement? And on her bed of all places? Had someone gotten lost? The package delivery company *did* hire people who were visually impaired—there'd been a big to-do about it on the news a few weeks before. That had to be it, she reasoned, because what other explanation was there? Surely, the dress couldn't be for her... or *could* it? Deciding to try it on, she scanned the basement to make sure she was alone. She then put it on, along with the shoes, and retrieved a cracked mirror from underneath her bed. After almost falling over from the shock of seeing her wild, frizzy hair—she usually avoided mirrors—she inspected the rest of herself and discovered that she actually had a figure. And her ashy complexion was gone; it was as though the pink from the dress was reflecting up onto her face.

Clunk, clunk, clunk.

"Hello!" Someone yelled from the stairs, their voice barely discernible over the washing machines. "I'm coming down! Make sure you're decent!"

Clunk, clunk, clunk.

It took a moment, but V realized it was Instructor Verin and her anger at him resurfaced. Scowling, she shoved the mirror under the bed and turned to meet him; she was far too upset to care whether or not he noticed what she was wearing. Seconds later, he clunked into her corner of the basement. He had a leather satchel strapped across his chest and a bucket stuck on each foot.

"Yes, that dress will do all right!" he said, shouting over the woosh, woosh, thump, thump, thumps. "It's quite an improvement if I say so myself! I have quite excellent taste at picking clothes, wouldn't you agree?"

V's scowl disappeared. "*You* got this dress for *me*?"

"Of course I did! I couldn't let you be seen wearing those other atrocious things you're always in! Besides, this dress will compliment your persona!"

V suddenly felt light-headed; in her entire life, no one had ever given her anything. And certainly nothing so... *nice*.

"Persona?"

"Yes!" Instructor Verin clunked over, brushing a speck of dust from her shoulder before holding up one of his bucketed feet. "Would you mind helping me get these off? They don't match my outfit!"

Still a bit light-headed, V nodded and did her best to remove the buckets without falling over or passing out.

"Thank you!" shouted Instructor Verin. "Now, come along, we haven't got all day!" He turned to leave and veered over to the nightstand where V had put his yellow book. "I've been looking for this! Good to see it's been taken care of!" Tucking it into his satchel, he headed for the stairs.

"Wait!" Tossing the buckets aside and grabbing her spatula, V hurried after him; despite her anger and frustration, he was still her only hope of leaving the school. "What's going on? Where are you going?"

"We!" Instructor Verin corrected over his shoulder. "Where are *we* going!"

"Okay, where are *we* going?"

"You'll see!"

V followed him up the stairs, through a maze of dark hallways, and out the crooked front doors of the school. Clapping, cheering, and several bright flashes, greeted her. Torn between covering her eyes or covering her ears (yes, her tiny basement corner *was* dismal and noisy, but she much preferred it to *this)* she tried to go back inside, but Instructor Verin stopped her.

"Turn around and just play along," he whispered.

V hesitantly lowered her hands and turned around. Lining the descending stone steps were at least twenty reporters with notepads, voice recorders, and cameras. Behind them, a pastel-rainbow spaceship was docked on the school's scraggly front lawn. Suddenly, her unusual conversation with Headmaster Baz and the appearance of the shiny bot were making sense. As were Instructor Verin's shenanigans with the makeup and apology paper; evidently, he was willing to do *anything* to find out what the headmaster was up to. But what did this have to do with Threka?

"Please tell me you didn't really do this," she whispered to the instructor from the corner of her mouth.

"I did, actually," he whispered back. "But we'll talk about it later. Play along, remember?" Smiling brightly, he stepped forward to meet the nearest reporter, who just happened to be a woman.

Barely acknowledging V, the reporter homed in on the instructor. "So, Xander Verin…" she smiled. "… is it alright if I call you Xander?"

"Of course," he replied.

The reporter's smile widened, and she flipped a lock of hair over her shoulder. "Xander, could you please tell me what it was that inspired a dashing instructor such as yourself to not only befriend someone with creampuffatosis, but to also be her assistant in the Baking Adventures Fun-Times-For-Everyone-All-The-Time Competition?"

"Cupcakitosis," corrected Instructor Verin.

"Right, cakepuffatosis." Still smiling, the reporter flipped her hair again.

"Cupcakitosis, actually. But in answer to your question, I have always felt that we should be doing more for our communities, especially for those who have challenges that most of us do not. V here…" Instructor Verin put an arm around V's shoulders. "…has a very debilitating disorder and what better way to help her than by letting her baking light shine in the greatest baking show ever to air in our galaxy?"

More clapping and cheering. More lights flashing.

V's head swirled from the commotion; was this really happening? She glanced at Instructor Verin who was answering more questions and visibly soaking up every bit of attention. It's happening, she thought, feeling faint. At her left, she heard a tromp! tromp! tromp! Turning her head towards the sound, she looked over the crowd and saw the shiny bot exit the spaceship. It then tromped across the lawn and up the stairs, only stopping when it got to her and Instructor Verin.

It was time to leave.

10

Nineteen years, seven months, and five days. That was how long V had lived at the Deluxe Worldmaker School for Worldmakers. As an infant, she'd been left on the doorstep, a note pinned to her diaper:

Dear Master Blacksmith,
Please give this baby a better life,
Thank you.

Alas, there were no master blacksmiths at the school. There *was* one in a nearby town, but according to law, V was property of the school the moment she'd been set down. Otherwise, she'd have been bustled off and would likely have grown up making things like horseshoes and shovels. Instead, she'd grown up making messes... and cleaning them.

She stared out the spaceship's window. Someone was speaking, but it was garbled into the background because all she could think about was leaving the school. For the first time in her life, she was *leaving the school!*

"V. V...? *V!*"

"What?" She looked at Instructor Verin, who was sitting beside her. Aside from the two of them, the passenger compartment was empty.

"Have you been listening to me? I've been telling you

some very important—"

"Do I have to go back?" she cut in.

"Go back?" He looked confused.

"*To the school*—do I have to go *back*?"

"Is it really necessary to discuss that right now? The competition is—"

"*Yes.*" She sucked in a shallow breath. Surely, her wish couldn't be coming true so easily, and without her even speaking to him about it.

Instructor Verin sighed. "Yes, you have to go back."

Exhaling, she looked down at her hands, her few seconds of elation fizzling. "But you can change that, right? I've helped you, now you can help me."

"I'm sorry, but it's not that easy."

"But you can still do it, right?" Her eyes shot to his. "After everything I've done for you? Not to mention you tricking me onto this show and telling the entire galaxy that I have cupcakitosis? You need to do *something*."

Another sigh. "All right. I'll see what I can do. But first, we have to find the connection to Threka."

This time, V didn't give in to the elation tugging at her insides. "Okay. How do we do that?"

"We bake. Actually, *you* bake because I don't know how to."

"But, I don't know how to bake either."

"V, you work in the kitchen."

"I *clean* the kitchen and stir porridge—Grula's the one who did all the baking."

"Then…" Instructor Verin rubbed his nose and seemed to be thinking. "Then, I guess we'll have to improvise." He opened his satchel and pulled out the yellow book.

"With that?" V's stomach twisted into a knot; the moment she'd taken the book off his desk she'd known it would only cause trouble. How could she have been so stupid?

"Yes."

"*How?*"

"I'm not sure, but there's got to be something in here..." He flipped through the pages until he reached the end. He then went back to the beginning and flipped through the pages again. "Have you by chance seen a white piece of paper?" He felt around his seat before searching underneath it.

Having a pretty good idea of what he was searching for, V shifted uncomfortably. "You, um, wouldn't be referring to Ooblick's worldmaker certificate, would you?"

Surprise flashed across Instructor Verin's face. It was immediately followed by horror. "You know about *Ooblick*?"

"Yeah—his certificate was in your book, and I wanted to know who he was, so I looked him up. It said he was probably dead because his home planet had been destroyed."

"What did you do with the certificate?"

"I put it back."

He flipped through the pages a third time. "It's not here," he said, setting the book aside. "I knew I should have put it somewhere else, and now it's lost! This is just about the worst thing that's ever happened to me!" He clapped both hands over his face and started crying.

Feeling a prick of guilt, V put a hand on his shoulder. Yes, she was still upset about the makeup and his deception with the apology paper, but that wasn't Ooblick's fault. Just like it wasn't Ooblick's fault that he was probably dead, or that the instructor had had his worldmaker certificate, which she'd obviously lost. "I'm really sorry," she said. "And I'm sorry for

Ooblick too, whoever he was."

"Why?" Instructor Verin sniffled and parted his fingers, looking out at her.

"Because I think he was a lot like me: not that great looking, no friends, horrible clothes…"

"You're right," he said, closing his fingers. "At least about Ooblick, only, he isn't dead—Ton wasn't actually his home world, it's just where he went to school. But if anyone finds out, my cover's blown."

"Why? It's not like he's around to tell anyone."

Instructor Verin sank down in his seat.

"It's not like Ooblick's around here, is he?" V prodded.

He sank down even lower.

The back of her neck prickled. "Don't tell me… that… *you…*?"

"Okay!" He wailed from behind his hands, this time sinking so low that he slid off his seat entirely and landed on the floor with a thud. "It's true! It's true! Just don't say it aloud!"

"*You* are Ooblick?" she hissed.

He nodded.

"But… Ooblick was so… *ugly*. You…" she scrambled to the floor and knelt at his side, prying his hands from his face, "…*you* aren't ugly at all."

"I know," he whimpered. "It's because I changed my nose. And my hair."

V tried to envision Ooblick as Instructor Verin, only with a different nose and different hair, but was unable to do so. "Why did you change your nose?"

"Do you really need to ask?"

"Okay, I get why you changed your nose, but what made

68

you do it?"

"After reading my certificate, I'm sure you've put it together that I'm a worldmaker?"

She nodded even though she hadn't consciously put it together until that moment. But now that she had, his mysterious cleanup of the pantry suddenly made sense.

"But I'm not a very good one," he admitted. "I can manipulate the elements, but if I try to make something from them, they turn straight to mush."

"Then how did you become certified?"

"My instructors didn't want me retaking their classes."

"And your nose?" As soon as V said the word *nose*, the instructor tried to cover his face again, but she tightened her grip on his hands.

"One of my schoolmates called me 'Mush Boy' and tripped me," he said pitifully. "My nose broke and I had to have surgery."

"Oh." V felt sorry for his pain, but not for his hideous nose, which thankfully, was no longer around. "You look great now, though."

"Thanks." Instructor Verin's lips wobbled. "But back to the certificate; you should know that if someone finds it and figures out who I really am, I'll be put to... to... *death!*"

11

"Put to *death*?" V exclaimed. "What do you mean, put to *death*?"

"Shhh! Not so loud!" hissed Instructor Verin. Still lying on the floor in a pitiful heap, he glanced at the cockpit door. "It said in the contract that if anyone enters the competition under false pretenses, they'll be *drowned* in a vat of *frosting*."

V was horrified. "That's terrible!" she whispered.

"I know," Instructor Verin whispered back with a sniffle.

"So, what do we do?" V asked tearfully. She wasn't one to give in to her emotions, but it really upset her that, despite the instructor's willingness to help, her dreams might never become real. And it was all her fault: if she'd just left that stupid yellow book alone... "If you die," she lamented, "I'll have to go back to the school, and I can't go back—I can't! I'm so sorry, this is all my fault!"

A few long seconds ticked by and Instructor Verin sniffled again. "You're right—you can't go back. No matter what happens to me, I promise that you will never go back to that school."

V wiped her nose with the hem of her dress and silently vowed to make sure he made it out of the competition alive. "Okay."

"Everything's going to work out, we just need to hope for the best and focus on winning this competition," he went on.

Seeming to have collected himself, he patted her knee and then reached into one of his pockets, pulling out a small piece of paper. "I made a 'To Do' list. It should prove very useful in helping us do that."

Rubbing the moisture from her eyes, V took the paper and looked it over:

1. Stay away from buckets.
2. Bake food.
3. Find connection to Threka.
4. Comb hair.
5. T. P.D.
6. Win competition.

It really *wasn't* helpful *or* useful, but she didn't want to insult the instructor on top of possibly getting him killed. "It looks like it tells us what to do, and what not to do—that's good. But what does T.P.D mean?"

Instructor Verin's cheeks turned pink, his eyes darting away. "Nothing. It means nothing."

V got the feeling there was something he wasn't telling her. "Okay. So, what about the baking?" She handed the paper back to him. "What information did they give you when you signed up?"

"Not much. Just that the competition will last two days, and we won't know what we're making until right before each baking session starts."

"So, we don't get time to practice?"

"No. I think the man said they're trying something new?"

"That's not good—we'll be the first ones sent home."

"Failure is not an option, V—we have to at *least* make it

to the last session."

"At *least*? That's going to take a miracle."

"Then we'll hope for a miracle."

Just then, the cockpit door slid open, and the shiny bot tromped out. "We have reached our destination," it announced.

"Wow!" V almost couldn't believe it. "That went by *really* fast. I mean, I had *no* idea how fast these things could go—we were only in here for like, *twenty minutes*!"

"Spaceships do travel quite speedily these days," said Instructor Verin with a smile.

A minute or so later, the two of them were following the bot off the ship and into a large room with metal walls and a metal ceiling. An anxious looking man wearing a pastel-rainbow suit was waiting for them outside the ship's door. Holding a pink and white cupcake in one of his hands, he was using his other hand to smooth a sparse comb-over.

"Welcome to Fooda," he said. "My name is Bon Munchi-Kumkwat, but you can call me Bon." He held the cupcake out to V. "This is for you."

She took it thinking that, maybe, this whole cupcakatosis thing wasn't going to be so bad after all. "Thank you."

"You're welcome," said Bon, looking more anxious than before. "You can eat it. In fact, you *should* eat it—the sooner the better."

She took a bite.

Noticeably relieved, he turned to Instructor Verin and lowered his voice, "This is our first time having someone like V with us and we really hope she can control her... *problem*."

"Oh, you don't need to worry about her," Instructor Verin replied. "She's very comparable."

Comparable? V thought doubtfully, between bites. That

doesn't sound right... Perhaps he meant something else, something like *competent* or *capable*...? She certainly hoped so.

Bon also looked doubtful. "Yes, well, down to business." He gestured to a large hover-bus painted in pastel-rainbow stripes. "We'd like to take the two of you on an air-tour of Delectabelia, the capital of Fooda. After, we'll go to the Blue Sparkle where you and the other competitors are staying. Dinner will be provided and there will be a briefing about the competition."

"Sounds great," said Instructor Verin. "What do you think, Vivi?"

V arched an eyebrow. "Vivi?"

"Yes—that's what you asked me to call you, remember?" He gave her a look that seemed to say, 'just play along.'

She resisted the urge to roll her eyes. "Oh yes, *now* I remember. And an air tour sounds great."

"Onto the hover-bus, then," said Bon. The watch on his wrist beeped and he excused himself, trotting a little way off.

Taking another bite of cupcake, V followed the instructor onto the hover-bus. The shiny bot tromped on behind her, sitting at the control panel in the front.

"Can I have some of your cupcake?" Instructor Verin whispered as V sat down beside him. Without waiting for an answer, he reached over and brushed a few fingers over the pink and white frosting.

"Hey! Why did you do that?"

"I just wanted a taste." After licking his fingers, he reached for the cupcake again.

"No." She held it as far off to the side of her as she could.

"You know, sharing would be the nice thing to do."

"Yeah, but you're not *sharing*, you're *taking*."

"Well, what else am I supposed to do? Bon didn't give me a cupcake, and I really want one."

"Then maybe you should try telling him that you have cupcakitosis, *too*."

"Mmm." Instructor Verin rubbed his nose. "Nope. As much as I want to, I can't. So, I'll just have to make do with yours."

Suddenly, the cupcake floated out of V's hand and her jaw dropped. A *floating* cupcake? She glanced at the instructor; he was looking very pleased with himself. "No!" Grabbing the cupcake, she shoved what was left of it into her mouth, paper wrapper and all.

Now it was Instructor Verin's jaw that dropped. "I can't believe you just did that!"

"I can't believe you did that, either!" said someone else.

V looked over at whoever had spoken and saw Bon climbing aboard the hover-bus. Her eyes widened; had he seen the floating cupcake? "Ooh camp bewewe wap?" she said through her enormous mouthful.

"The wrapper!" he croaked. "I can't believe you put that wrapper in your mouth!" Turning a sickly shade of green, he grabbed a trash bin out from underneath the control panel and vomited into it.

12

"I don't see what the big deal is," V whispered to Instructor Verin. "It was just a cupcake wrapper." A few rows ahead of them, Bon was lying on the floor of the hover-bus crying pitifully for his 'fluffy white cat' named 'Giblit.'

"If you'd just given me your cupcake, he'd be fine right now," Instructor Verin whispered back.

"Seriously?" quipped V. "If you'd just left my cupcake *alone*, none of this would have happened."

"If you'd just let me have a bite, then none of this would have happened either and we would *still* have a tour of Delectebilia. But now, we've got no tour and I've yet to get a single bite of cupcake," he sulked.

"If you'd just kept your cupcake floating abilities to yourself, *none* of this would have happened."

"Well, how else was I supposed to get some cupcake?"

"I don't know, but you can't just go around making things float. What if Bon had seen you? You've got to be more *careful*."

"You're right." The corners of Instructor Verin's mouth turned down. "I got carried away showing off; it just feels so nice not having to hide that part of myself from everyone any more." He let out a long, despondent sounding sigh. "It won't happen again. At least, not around anyone but you." He pulled a comb out of his pocket and ran it through his hair.

Letting out her own sigh—one of bewilderment at how someone could be so reckless when their life was on the line—V turned to look out the window and noticed that they were slowing down, descending onto a large courtyard. To one side of it was a tall, sparkly-blue building, a pastel-rainbow teepee, and a water fountain. To the other side of it was a street crowded with thousands of people.

After circling the courtyard a few times, the hover-bus finally landed. As soon as the door opened, Bon was up, stumbling down the steps.

"We'd better get off too," said Instructor Verin. Extending a hand, he helped V to her feet and the two of them exited the hover-bus. Right outside the door was a disheveled young man wearing a pastel-rainbow suit and a matching necktie. On the lapel of his jacket was a tag that read, 'Hello, my name is Rainbow Jon.'

"Welcome to the Blue Sparkle," Rainbow Jon said. "This is for you." He held a cupcake out to V, but before she had a chance to take it, Bon stumbled over and grabbed it. Ripping off the wrapper, he ran to the water fountain and tossed it in before bringing the cupcake back to Rainbow Jon.

"What was that about?" Rainbow Jon asked as Bon staggered off. He offered the cupcake to V once more.

She took it, but wasn't thrilled about its newly, somewhat smooshed, condition. Or by the fact that it had passed through two sets of hands without its wrapper. But, she *was* hungry, *and* she had to keep up appearances.

"The cupcake wrapper Vivi put in her mouth while we were on the hover-bus," said Instructor Verin.

Rainbow Jon nodded. "That makes sense; here on Fooda, cupcake wrappers and parchment paper are made of recycled, used, toilet paper. That's why Bon and I only eat at Guido's, the little bistro down the street. Nothing they make requires either of those things."

V, who'd just barely taken a bite of the cupcake, choked and spat her mouthful onto the ground. The remaining cupcake she threw as far away from herself as she could, which just happened to be to the other side of the courtyard.

The onlooking crowds cheered.

"I knew it!" a man with spiky, red hair shouted. "I knew it! Cupcakes make excellent fertilizer! My company is going to be a success!"

More cheers followed.

Instructor Verin made a gagging sound. "Did you just say that the cupcake wrappers and parchment paper on Fooda are made from recycled, used, toilet paper?"

"Cupcake wrappers for sure," said Rainbow Jon. "Mr. Dolop insists on recycling everything here. But don't tell anyone I told you—it's supposed to be a secret."

***

"I don't feel so good," said V. "I can't believe I have to constantly be eating something that's wrapped in used toilet paper." She now understood why Bon had gotten so sick—he'd known Palfrey Dolop's dirty little secret. And yet, if it really *was* a secret, why had that red-haired man shouted something about cupcakes making excellent fertilizer?

"Recycled," said Instructor Verin, sounding a bit sick himself. "That's not as bad as *not* recycled."

The elevator they were riding in lurched to a stop and the doors slid open.

"That's it down there," said Rainbow Jon, pointing down a hallway. "That's your rooms."

Instructor Verin poked his head out of the elevator. "But there's only one door."

"That's right—*that's* your rooms."

"But there's only one door," Instructor Verin said again.

"Yes, your rooms are actually together."

V's forehead wrinkled. "Together? How can separate rooms be together?"

"Mr. Palfrey has asked that the competitors share rooms until the remodel is finished," explained Rainbow Jon.

Instructor Verin's brow furrowed. "The remodel?"

"Yes," said Rainbow Jon. "If you need anything, just holler. But as I'm the only bellhop, cook, and janitor, it might take some time for me to get to you, *if* I even hear you." He promptly shooed V and the instructor out into the hallway, the elevator doors closing behind them. Half a minute later, they were standing in their "rooms".

"Oh no," said Instructor Verin.

"What's wrong?" V asked. She scanned her surroundings. The sparkly, blue walls were bare, as were the windows, and the light fixtures were gone. The furniture consisted of two cots set close together, and at the foot of the cots, a wooden crate that was turned upside down. On top of the crate was a small telly. Everything was clean and the scent of lemons lingered in the air. "Wow, this is nice."

"No." Instructor Verin shook his head. "There is nothing 'wow' or 'nice' about this. Everything's wrong; where am I supposed to lounge? Where am I supposed to gaze at myself for an hour every morning? Where will I put my shoes?"

"On the floor?" V guessed.

"No—a shoe tree, of which there is none in sight." He pursed his lips. "Doesn't this seem strange to you? A show this popular should be pulling in billions by the day. You'd think they'd offer us more than this, even during a remodel."

"I guess, but it's a hundred times better than my corner in the basement; it has walls, windows, a telly, carpet..." V slipped off her shoes, setting her bare feet on the thick, blue shag. It was like stepping onto a pile of cotton balls. "Plus, I don't have to worry about floods, or raccoons," she said, wandering over to the nearest window and looking outside. Far below in the courtyard, the crowds were going wild as two people stepped off another hover-bus. They appeared to be male and were very, very tall. "Instructor Verin, come look at this," she said. "Down there."

"Mmm?" He walked to the window and leaned over V's shoulder. "I'm having a hard time being impressed by any of this; you'd think that Palfrey Dolop, renowned worldmaker, would care more about showing off his money. To me, this speaks to a lack of money. Especially the part about recycling toilet paper."

"Stop thinking about that and just look." She pointed at the two men. "When was the last time you saw someone that tall?"

"A few days ago."

"Exactly."

"Exactly what?"

"Exactly, as in *they* could be the men we saw with Headmaster Baz at the school. It would explain the baking application."

"Nah, that would be too easy. I bet it's that Rohem Prince, Seff Pip, and his bodyguard; Rohems are notoriously tall."

"But the men we saw could have been Rohems too, right? You did say the gibberish they were speaking sounded like Rohemish. And you also said they would have pulled off our ears and noses, which is what Rohems are known for doing."

"Yes, I did say that, but only because they were so big. Besides, Rohema's in the middle of a war right now—why would anyone from there waste time going to a rundown school on a dinky little planet in the middle of nowhere?" Instructor Verin stared out the window a moment longer before letting out a 'humph.' Going to one of the cots, he sat down and flipped on the telly. A commercial was playing,

"Get your own pet-mess vacuum, get it now… Get your own pet-mess vacuum, we'll show you how…"

"I swear that's the only commercial I see or hear any more," V said, stepping away from the window. She went to the other cot and sat down. Moments later, the jingle ended, and the news flashed on, showing a picture of herself and Instructor Verin standing on the front steps of the Deluxe Worldmaker School For Worldmakers. A newsman with green hair was speaking,

"We have just learned that our final contestant in the Adventures of Fun Times… um, Baking… Everyone Show… is a less fortunate young lady known only as 'V.' With a history of endless stupors, donut binges, and random outbursts of stupid jokes, one very big-hearted instructor took compassion on her and entered her into the competition in hopes that it would give her something to live for. In his own words…"

"Donut binges? Stupid jokes? What does that have to do with me?" V wondered aloud. "And what is the Adventures of Fun Times Um Baking Show?"

"Shhh!" Instructor Verin pointed to the telly as the picture changed to a recording of him and a woman with a microphone.

"What was it that made a gorgeous instructor such as yourself take pity on a frizzy-haired cleaning girl?" the woman with the microphone asked.

"Well, there's just far too much need and want in this galaxy and where I've been given so much, I wanted to give back," said the Instructor Verin on the telly.

"Incredible," replied the woman with the microphone. "What a strong, gallant specimen of a man you are. My name's Palea Lolin and here's my phone number if you ever want me to ask you more questions." She handed him a card before a woman with pink hair shoved her down the stairs.

"My turn," said the pink-haired woman. "So, how many girlfriends do you have and how do they feel about this venture you're embarking on?"

Mostly, V had blocked out what happened on the school's steps, but now that she was watching it, the absurdity of certain individuals' actions came rushing back. "Can we turn this off?" she asked. "I don't think I can handle the colossal amount of stupidity that's about to be broadcast."

"Quiet," hissed Instructor Verin. "It's just getting to the good part."

"Just one," said the Instructor Verin on the telly. "And she has no idea—it will be quite the surprise when she sees this."

"Is there any possibility she'll be so angry with you as to break off your relationship?" the pink-haired woman asked hopefully.

"I'll be his new girlfriend!" someone in the crowd shouted.

The pink-haired woman started to shout back but was

tackled by a lady wearing a frog hat. Immediately after, a mob of women swarmed the frog-hat lady, one of them falling backward into the camera.

"Ouch!" someone exclaimed as the camera clattered to the ground.

Having seen enough, V turned off the telly.

"Hey," said Instructor Verin. "Why did you do that?"

"Did you not see what was happening? And how absurdly those women were behaving?"

"But—"

"And why didn't you tell Ursa you were coming on the show?" V demanded to know.

Instructor Verin sighed before dramatically flopping back on his cot. "Because I knew she'd try to stop me," he said, staring up at the ceiling, "she doesn't like it when I exercise my independence. Besides…" he reached into his shirt pocket and pulled out a key. "… I didn't get permission to borrow this from her."

"Seriously?" V was mystified. "You didn't tell her you were coming on the show because you took a *key* of hers without asking?"

"Correct. And by me not telling her, I was hoping to delay her finding out that it's missing."

"I don't understand."

"Then listen to what I'm saying."

"I am and it's not making sense."

"All right then, I'll try to simplify it for you: the key belongs to a friend of hers and if she knew I was coming on the show, she'd have wanted to come too, and would have brought it with her."

V tilted her head to the side. "So, you didn't tell her about the key because you didn't want her to come with us?"

"Precisely." Instructor Verin's gaze shifted to V. "I wouldn't have minded the key coming, but I can't have Ursa here because she'd know something was going on."

"Okay, so you don't want her interfering, but what does the key have to do with that?"

"Everything," he insisted. "This is the key to Palfrey Dolop's penthouse."

13

V was incredulous. "You're joking."

"No, I'm not," swore Instructor Verin, his dark hair static-clinging to the coarse fabric of the cot. "Palfrey Dolop lives in this building and if he's tied up in what's going on, then this key is going to help us find out how."

"You mean if he's tied up in the baking show? Doesn't he *own* the show?"

"Well, yes... but remodel or not, you have to admit there's something fishy going on around here: where's all the furniture? Why does he only have one person to cook, clean, and wait on guests? Where is all of his money going?"

"I don't know."

"And doesn't that strike you as odd? What if he's in cahoots with Headmaster Baz and the two of them are working with Threka? What if that's what the application was for?"

"But Headmaster Baz isn't here, and we still don't know *who* the application was for."

"Which is why *we* are here and why I brought *this*." Instructor Verin waved the key through the air.

Feeling a headache coming on, V rubbed both sides of her forehead. "So, why does Ursa have Palfrey Dolop's penthouse key?"

"You know, Vivi, I wondered that too, until I saw a picture of them standing together in front of a giant billboard that read,

'Family and Friends Make the Best Business Partners.' That's when I realized they were probably friends and likely also business partners."

"Okay…" She let out a long, bewildered breath. "So, you took the key because you think Palfrey might have some connection to Threka through Ursa?"

"Correct."

"But Ursa's got to know you're here—it's all over the news."

"Not so. She's at a spa getting her total-body, putrefied fish-skin wrap. It's a forty-eight-hour process."

"Oh, yuck!" V exclaimed. "Why would she do that? Come to think of it, why would *anyone* do that?"

"Ursa said it's something to do with staying youthful," he replied with a shrug.

"Probably because she's in her *nineties*." V scrunched up her nose.

"Is she really?" Instructor Verin's eyebrows shot up.

"That's what they said on the news."

"Wow, I had *no* idea. But if that wrap is what's keeping her so youthful, then perhaps I should look into it."

"You're not really thinking of getting one too, are you?"

"A little… Okay, yes," he admitted. "But I suppose we should refocus on our current predicament."

"How?"

"With this." He waved the key again.

"We're breaking into Palfrey's penthouse?"

"No, not we—*you*."

"*Me*?" V snorted. "I don't think so."

"But if he finds you, you can start doing something crazy like throwing those cesspool cupcakes around. Or you could yell terrible things at the top of your lungs. Me, on the other hand…" Instructor Verin ran a hand over his static-riddled locks. "Well, he'd know right away something was wrong."

"But I'm not a real spy," she objected.

"Maybe not, but if anyone can find something suspicious, it's *you*."

"You don't know that."

"I do, actually—you've got a natural flare for snooping. You found Ooblick's worldmaker certificate, didn't you?"

"Yeah, but that wasn't hard—you weren't exactly subtle in your choice of hiding place."

"And no doubt Palfrey's got some not-so-subtle hiding places, *too*."

V bit her lip and thought about how wonderful it would be to not go back to the school. "Fine, I'll do it."

Knock. Knock.

Instructor Verin sat up, his hair poofing out into an almost perfect halo around his head. "Now, who could that be?" Returning the key to his pocket, he went to the door and opened it. Rainbow Jon was standing in the hallway, dripping with sweat.

"Dinner… ready," he panted, leaning on the door frame. "Down… lobby. Dining hall… on left."

Attempting to pat down his hair, Instructor Verin said, "You came all this way to tell us? Why didn't you just call? And why are you so sweaty?"

"No… phones… Dolop… sold… Elevators too… going… now."

Hearing some clanging noises coming from outside, V got up and hurried to the window. A big, rectangular truck was parked in the courtyard and a metal box that looked remarkably like an elevator was being loaded into the back of it. "I think he's right," she said, first looking at Instructor Verin and then at Rainbow Jon. "But why would Mr. Dolop do that?"

"Don't... know," puffed Rainbow Jon.

"Hmm," said Instructor Verin, sounding perplexed. "In that case, you should promptly move us to one of the lower floors."

Rainbow Jon shook his head. "No. Mr. Dolop...adamant. This be... rooms... other rooms... walls... gone."

"The walls are *gone*?"

"Yes."

"Well then," Instructor Verin tried to pat down his hair again, "can you at least tell me what's for dinner?"

"Cake... Cupcakes..."

"Is there nothing else to eat? Nothing that involves cupcake wrappers or parchment paper?"

"No."

"Then we will be dining elsewhere, and Vivi will need at least a dozen cupcakes delivered to our roo—"

"NOOOOOOOO!" Rainbow Jon abruptly wailed. And without any sort of explanation, he ran off down the hallway.

14

V rubbed a few fingers over the handle of her metal spatula. "Why do I have to carry this around with me wherever I go?" she asked.

"Because it's part of your persona," said Instructor Verin. "You have to convince the other competitors that you really *do* have cupcakitosis."

"Ugh, cupcakes…" Her stomach flip-flopped. "How am I supposed to be convincing if I can't eat them?"

"Good question; maybe you could pretend to eat them, but throw them over your shoulder instead?"

"I thought you said I was supposed to be *convincing*. This is all your fault—choosing cupcakes, *cupcakatosis*."

"I know, but at the time it seemed so perfect; when we first met, you were eating a cupcake, remember? The one that got smashed onto my nose?"

"Oh, yeah…" V's cheeks flushed with embarrassment, but she didn't worry about Instructor Verin seeing her because the closet they were standing in didn't have any lightbulbs and was therefore dark. And empty—aside from the bucket he'd narrowly managed to avoid with her help. It really wasn't the best place to talk, but he'd insisted they come up with a strategy for the competition, and that they do so in private. So far, their strategy, or rather, *his* strategy, was to win, and the 'To Do' list was the means by which they would do so. "Maybe we should go," said V. "We've been in here a while and my legs aren't feeling so wobbly any more after hiking down forty-seven floors. Can you believe it? What's Palfrey Dolop thinking, putting us all the way at the top of the Blue Sparkle and then selling all the elevators?"

"Excellent question. Let's go find out, shall we?"

Less than a minute later, they were standing in the dining hall. Completely devoid of furniture, the walls were gone exposing several concrete pillars. A lit chandelier dangled from what was left of the ceiling. Right below it, four people, and a cloud with arms and legs, were sitting around a blanket piled with an assortment of cakes, cupcakes, and pancakes.

"Oh, look," Instructor Verin said, sounding sick. "Dinner."

Feeling a bit sick herself, V trained her attention on the people and cloud; if only Rainbow Jon hadn't run off so unexpectedly, she and the instructor might have questioned him further: had he said 'no' to them leaving and eating elsewhere? Or just to bringing cupcakes to their room?

"And now," the cloud was softly saying in a low-pitched voice, "close your eyes and breathe in the blessed scent of serenity. For here, at the Baking Adventures Fun-Times-For-Everyone-All-The-Time Competition, we are all serene. Still as a sparkling lake of clear, blue water."

The people at the blanket closed their eyes and breathed in.

"Very good," said the cloud. "Now open your eyes and feel the air in the room swirling around you, coaxing you to your feet."

Very slowly, everyone got to their feet.

"Now stretch both arms high above your head," the cloud

continued. "And gently spin around…"

"Hey!" said a little girl with braided hair. "Look, more competitors!"

None of the other people seemed to notice, or care… except for the cloud.

"Stay here my friends, and continue your breathing exercises while I greet some *new* friends." The cloud stepped away from the blanket and headed towards V and Instructor Verin.

On closer inspection, the cloud wasn't an actual cloud, *he* was a *man*. White spandex covered his arms and legs, and covering his head, shoulders, torso, and thighs was a round, fluffy cotton costume that looked remarkably like a real cloud. A small opening near the top revealed a face that was partially hidden behind a pair of rose-tinted glasses.

Suddenly, Instructor Verin put his hand in front of V's eyes. "For all that is good and delicious on this planet—I am *not* referring to cupcakes—*don't look*," he whispered.

A few seconds later, the man in the cloud costume stopped in front of them. "Hello," he said. "My name is Stuarp."

Instructor Verin made a weird choking sound. "Right, um… Hello, Stuarp."

V stayed silent; for the moment she could only see the tips of Stuarp's glossy, white shoes.

"The two of you must be Xander Verin and V," Stuarp said. "I saw all about you on the news. You're V's assistant," he said, clearly speaking to the instructor. "And you, V, have a disorder that makes you eat raspberry tarts all day long or else you start kicking dogs."

"Uh…" She was about to tell him that he'd gotten his facts wrong, when Instructor Verin made the choking sound again.

"Yes, I'm Xander Verin and this is Vivi, but I'm the only one who can call her that. What can we do for you?"

"I just came over to say 'Welcome'," said Stuarp. "The two of you make number six, so now, only the prince and his bodyguard are left. While we wait for them, would you like to join us for some breathing exercises?" His voice lowered. "This crowd is a bit excitable, if you get my meaning. They were nearly at each other's throats before I got here, so I thought it best to implement something to keep them calm. You really should come join us—it might offend them and incite dangerous actions if you don't."

"When you put it like that, we'd be more than happy to," Instructor Verin said in a strained voice. "Wouldn't we, Vivi?"

Wondering what in the worlds was going on, she said hesitantly, "Sure?"

"Oh good," Stuarp exhaled. "Come along then."

V watched Stuarp's shoes disappear from her limited field of view.

"I'm going to lower my hand now," whispered Instructor Verin, lowering his hand. "And I highly recommend *not* looking at Stuarp."

V's eyes went to his ashen face. "Why not?" she asked. "And why did you cover my eyes?"

"Didn't you see what he was dressed up as?"

"A cloud?"

"Yes, but not just any cloud—he's a *Kloud* with a capital K. They're a bunch of fanatics who believe clouds are endangered and that it's their job to save them. I got attacked by one my first year at Ton Worldmaker University. She pinned me to the ground and yanked out handfuls of my hair." He shuddered and tenderly touched the side of his head. "It was horrifying."

V wasn't sure 'horrifying' was the right word. 'Painful' seemed a little more on point. "Why did she attack you?"

"Because I looked at her. Well, *Ooblick* looked at her."

"That's it?"

"Yes."

"That doesn't seem like a very good reason. Even if it *was* Ooblick's face she saw."

"Obviously, she didn't need a better reason than that. So, now, whenever I see a Kloud, I *don't* look at them, and you shouldn't either."

Instructor Verin's face had lost so much color that V worried he would pass out—but she couldn't let that happen; he might not be much of a strategist, but he was all she had, and there was no way she was going through any part of this competition without him. Suddenly, an idea popped into her head. "The bucket!"

"The bucket?"

"Yes! Wait here!" She ran from the room and quickly returned with the bucket from the closet, plopping it on his head. "How's that?"

"I can't see anything."

"That's the point—now you don't have to worry about Stuarp. Even if he's right in front of you, you don't have to look at him." She silently added that the bucket would help her keep the instructor safe just in case someone found his worldmaker certificate and somehow managed to put two and two together.

"Oh! That's brilliant, Vivi! Thank you!"

"You're welcome," she said, with a smile.

"Come along, new friends!" Stuarp called. "Everyone's

waiting!

Spatula in one hand, V wrapped her other hand around Instructor Verin's arm and guided him to the blanket where the other competitors were still spinning around. Just as they got there, an old woman with a cane fell over. Stuarp rushed to her side.

"Are you okay Laquat?" he asked, helping her up.

"Help! Help! I'm being robbed!" the purple-haired woman shrieked. "This cloud is trying to steal my diamond sweater and ruby tooth!"

"No, I'm—"

"Yes, you are!" She swung her cane back and forth, hitting herself in the head and falling over again.

"Oh dear," said Stuarp. He pressed a few fingers to the side of her throat. "She's still alive, just knocked herself out." He returned to his spot in the circle. "You can all stop spinning now. We don't want anyone else getting hurt."

Slowly, the other competitors came to a stop, except for the little girl who'd noticed V and Instructor Verin. "But I don't want to stop spinning," she said.

"Just for a moment," said Stuarp. "Just until you introduce yourself to our new friends. Keep your arms above your head though. In fact, everyone, let's all keep our arms above our heads." He looked pointedly at V and Instructor Verin.

As the instructor couldn't seem to hear over the bubbly tune he'd started humming, V helped him raise his arms before raising her own.

"Why don't you go first, Elba?" Stuarp said to the little girl. "Say your name and then something you love."

Elba stopped spinning but was actively wiggling around. "I'm Elba," she said. "And I love chocolate chips on my spaghetti. I'm also this year's youngest competitor—nine years old! And the other day while I was in the swimming pool, my swimsuit—"

"Thank you," Stuarp cut in. "Let's move on and give the others a chance to introduce themselves."

Elba's eyes narrowed and her lips trembled. Her small hands clenched into fists.

"And you are now free to spin in some more circles!" Stuarp quickly said.

Elba's face brightened right up. "Hooray!" In a matter of seconds, she was spinning around the room like a top.

Stuarp let out a relieved sounding sigh. "Okay, let's continue—Truj, go ahead."

V looked at the next person in the circle: short hair, thick eyebrows, lumpy body, loose fitting clothes... Her forehead wrinkled in puzzlement; was Truj a man? Or a woman?

"My name is Truj," said Truj. "And I love flowers."

"Very nice. Thank you for sharing." Stuarp looked at the spot beside Truj and a short, plump man stepped forward.

"Name's Ha," said the man. "Not Han, or Harold, or Sam, just Ha. And if you call me anything else...." He shook a clenched fist.

"Okay, there. Let's calm down," said Stuarp. "No one's going to call you anything other than—"

"How about Honky Wonky Tonky Donkey Willy Wally Doodle Dolly?" Elba called from the other side of the dining hall.

Ha's face turned bright red. "How dare you!" he roared. Grabbing a cupcake from the blanket, he hurled it at Elba, hitting her in the face.

A blood-curdling scream filled the room.

"That's what you get you puny monster!" Ha shouted. He reached for another cupcake, but Stuarp grabbed his arm.

"No, Ha, don't do something you'll regret later. Let's discuss this like the mature adults we are."

"You're right." Yanking his arm out of Stuarp's hand, Ha grabbed another cupcake, smashing it on Stuarp's face before gathering an entire armful and sprinting after Elba.

"Food fight!" Truj yelled. He or she picked up a pink cake and threw it at Ha, but it missed, hitting Stuarp in the legs.

Elba, with a cupcake on her face, and several more splattered across her chest and back, spun over to the blanket and grabbed the pancakes, lobbing them at anyone and everyone.

Laquat, who'd awakened from all the ruckus, was back on her feet, swinging her cane at the assortment of flying cakes.

Stuarp, who'd taken to frantically running around and waving his arms through the air, was calling out things like, "Arms above your head! Breathe! Spin in a circle! Close your eyes and... No, Truj, don't do *that*!" He raced over to Truj who was smearing handfuls of cake onto the floor.

Meanwhile, everything was happening so fast that V was struggling to keep up. Her first instinct was to run like mad for the door, but, as she'd just witnessed, sudden movements only seemed to increase the lunacy of the other competitors. "We need to go," she hissed to Instructor Verin, who still had his arms in the air and was humming another bubbly tune. Pulling one of his arms down and tightly gripping it just above the elbow, she steadily backed towards the door. "Perhaps, if we go slow enough, they won't notice us leaving..."

"Traitors!" Laquat screeched. "Where do you think you're going? Bring back my emerald tooth!"

At first, V didn't know who Laquat was speaking to... until the old woman hobbled towards her with astounding speed. "Run!" she yelled. Pulling Instructor Verin with her, she ran for the door, but Ha sprinted over and wacked the bucket off Instructor Verin's head. A split second later, a yellow bundt cake hit the instructor in the face, knocking him to the floor. "Instructor Verin!" V dropped her spatula and bent down to help him up, but he was out cold.

"Treacherous thieves!" Laquat screeched, hobbling over and hitting V with her cane. "Where is it? Where's my opal tooth?"

Realizing it was useless to try and move the instructor on her own, and seeing as Laquat wasn't going to be any help, V scrambled to her feet and ran towards the door. "I'll come back for you, Instructor Verin! I promise!" she shouted over her shoulder. But she wasn't looking where she was going, and next thing she knew, she was slamming face-first into the front of someone very, very tall.

15

"You, okay?" whispered a gruff voice.

Blinking through bleary eyes, V saw a man hovering over her: light hair, dark eyebrows, a black patch covering the spot on his face where his nose should have been...

"I must make sure my wife is okay," the man went on. "Although, no one can know—it was a secret marriage, and my prince would not approve."

A waft of cinnamon tickled the inside of V's nose. "What?" she mumbled. But by then, the man was gone, a crumbly, yellow face appearing in his place. One of the crumbles dropped into her mouth. "Lemon?" She licked her lips.

"Yes, lemon bundt cake," said the crumbly, yellow face. "Due to the shape it once had, I'm ninety-nine point nine-nine-nine percent certain there was no parchment paper involved in its making. It's quite tasty, so I keep scraping it off my face and into my mouth."

"Instructor Verin?" V croaked.

"The one and only." The crumbly, yellow face smiled and more crumbles rained down on V.

"How's she doing?" Someone who sounded like Stuarp asked.

"I don't know," Instructor Verin said, hurriedly putting on his bucket. "How are you doing, Vivi?"

"Well… like I just ran into a wall… except it wasn't a wall, it was a man…? I think…?" As she rubbed her forehead, a cloud came into view. "Hi, Stuarp."

"Hello, V," said the cloud, looking pleased. "I'm glad to see you're conscious. Perhaps we should sit you up and see about getting you to your feet? The briefing will be starting soon. Oh, and here's your spatula."

After some gentle coaxing and a few short bouts of dizziness, V was on her feet with Instructor Verin's arm around her shoulders for support. The dining hall had fallen into a lull as the other competitors were either taking naps, eating cake, or creating murals on the floor with frosting.

"Look over there," Instructor Verin whispered. Peeking out from under his bucket, he gave V's shoulder a light squeeze. "That's Kesh Yib, the prince's bodyguard."

She followed his gaze to an enormously tall, broad-chested man with a nose patch—the same man who'd hovered over her earlier and whispered things about his wife. Currently, he was being dragged by Elba over to the blanket where the little girl began a quest of getting him to eat the remnants of a chocolate cake. He refused, until Elba's face scrunched up into a frightening expression.

"Are you sure he isn't one of the men we saw with Headmaster Baz?" V asked.

"Absolutely. What kind of bodyguard would leave his prince during a war?"

"But what if the prince went with him?"

"Of course, I went with him," said a deep voice.

Startled, V turned her head to the side. Towering over her was none other than Prince Seff Pip. Her cheeks flushed with heat; just how long had he been standing there, listening in on her and Instructor Verin's conversation? And just how much had he overheard with only one ear? Her eyes flickered to the bubbly looking scar on the right side of his head.

"Sorry, I didn't mean to embarrass you," he said. "I just wanted to make sure you were okay after your collision with Kesh."

"Oh… I'm okay… ", V said, shifting uncomfortably.

"I'm glad to hear that, but if you start feeling woozy, don't hesitate to get some rest, all right?"

She nodded.

He smiled. "I'm Prince Seff Pip, but you can call me Prince Seff."

"Hi, Prince Seff. I'm V."

"Nice to meet you, V. I look forward to getting to know you better—it seems that the two of us have quite a bit in common."

"Really?" To say she was surprised, was a bit of an understatement; what could *she* have in common with a *prince*?

"Yes, I too have an ailment that requires me to regularly eat a certain type of food," he explained. "Not cupcakes, mind you. And I don't start yelling horrible things at people, but my symptoms are just as debilitating."

V didn't know what to say, much less think; should she be happy that she wasn't alone in her "suffering"? Or should she feel guilty about her deception? Was the prince telling her the truth? Or was he merely poking fun at her?

Prince Seff smiled again. "It was nice to meet you. Now, if you'll excuse me, I must save my friend from death by cake and little girls who have horrid tempers and absolutely no manners." He nodded politely before walking over to Kesh and Elba, calmly inserting himself between them. Red-faced and screaming, the little girl pounded on his legs with her fists. In response, he picked her up by the feet and dangled her upside down.

"That was a most interesting conversation," said Instructor Verin, who was still peeking out from under his bucket. Letting go of V's shoulder, he bent over, tsk, tsk, tsking and tapping his cake-splattered shoes. "I wonder if Rainbow Jon knows how to clean these…"

Scccrrrreeeeeeaaaaaaakkkk!

Clamping both hands over her ears, V spun around in search of the offending sound, which she soon found at the back of the dining hall, emanating from a black box on the ground. Standing beside the box was Bon. No longer a sickly shade of green, he had a fluffy, white cat perched on his shoulder. If she remembered the balding man's cries on the hover-bus correctly, the cat's name was Giblit.

The high-pitched squeak sounded again, but quickly dissipated as Bon picked up a microphone from behind the black box and began speaking into it. "Can everyone hear me?" he asked.

The competitors stopped what they were doing and a disharmonious chorus of "yesses" echoed through the room.

"Good." Bon warily glanced at each of the competitors. "Now, as most of you know, my name is Bon, and I am here to welcome you to the Baking Adventures Fun-Times-For-Everyone-All-The-Time Competition. For those of you who are avid fans of the show, no doubt you've noticed some significant differences in this week's competition, but there's good reason as the show is undergoing a remodel—hence the lack of furniture and walls. But not to worry, Rainbow Jon and

I will do everything in our power to keep you comfortable."

Rainbow Jon stumbled through a nearby doorway and fell face first onto the floor. "I'm okay!" he said, rolling to his back. "I'm okay! Just need to take a little nap." He closed his eyes and started snoring.

"I'll ask him about my shoes after he's done taking his nap," Instructor Verin whispered to V.

A few snores later, Rainbow Jon jolted awake and jumped to his feet. "Nap time's over," he said, running from the room. Completely missing the open doorway, he ran into a pillar of concrete, but quickly righted himself, successfully exiting through the doorway that time.

"I suppose I'll have to wait until he comes back," sighed the instructor.

Meanwhile, Bon, who'd been carrying on as if nothing had happened, was saying, "There have also been a few other changes, so, during this time of transition, the regular judges will not be with us. Instead, the beloved creator of the show, Palfrey Dolop, will be your judge."

As though on cue, a smiling Palfrey Dolop entered the dining hall. "Welcome! Welcome!" he said, striding over to Bon and artfully slipping the microphone from his hands. "So glad to be here with all of you! And it does look as though you've been having a bit of fun, doesn't it?" His light-blue eyes scanned the room.

Truj was swirling a handful of frosting onto a pillar of concrete. Ha was guardedly watching the worldmaker from behind two fistfuls of pineapple cake. Laquat had hobbled over to Bon and was insisting that Giblit was really her long-lost Grannie Upsha, who'd stolen her garnet tooth and opal nose ring. Prince Seff was still holding Elba upside down by her feet. Kesh was glowering, his gloved hands balled into fists at his side. Stuarp was sitting cross-legged on the floor, and Instructor Verin was back inside his bucket.

"Let's get down to business," said Palfrey, an amused expression on his face. "As you all know, the competition takes place inside the teepee, but, as Bon has already informed you, there have been some temporary changes. As such, we will only have eight contestants this week instead of sixteen, making it so there will be only six bakes—three tomorrow and three the following day. As always, every bake but the last one, someone will be sent home. Now, on the telly, you see the competitors leaving peacefully, but as this is hardly ever the case off camera, we have employed one of our bots to escort cut competitors from the show." He paused, his eyes scanning the room again. When they landed on V, he smiled, his straight, white teeth gleaming in the chandelier light. "Are there any questions?"

"Yes," barked Ha. "Where's the lemon-strawberry cake? It's my absolute favorite and I demand to be given some!"

At the same time, Laquat wildly swung her cane through the air and screeched, "Mr. Palfrey, will you tell this bonehead to give me back my Grannie Upsha? She's stolen some very valuable items from me!"

Clutching Giblit to his chest and looking terrified, Bon dodged the old lady's cane and bolted past her.

"Stop! Thief!" Laquat screamed, hobbling after him.

"Wait!" Elba hollered. "I want to go too! Chasing the man with hardly any hair looks fun!"

Following a shrug from Kesh, Prince Seff let go of Elba. The little girl crashed to the floor, but quickly bounced to her feet and joined Laquat in chasing Bon around the room.

"Hey! Wait for me!" Truj exclaimed, loping after them.

"Me too!" bellowed Ha.

V pulled Instructor Verin out of the way as the five people and Giblit barreled past. She looked at Palfrey, hoping he would stop the madness, but he just smiled at her again before looking at the other competitors.

"No other questions? Great! I will turn the time back to you to mingle and eat. Just don't stay up too late! We want you bright-eyed and bushy-tailed tomorrow morning!" Palfrey set the microphone on the floor and left the dining hall.

V shook her head in disbelief. What was wrong with him? First the elevators, and now this? Was he really okay with letting the other competitors run around like a bunch of maniacs?

"Did you hear that?" Instructor Verin abruptly asked from inside his bucket.

"Hear what?" asked V.

"I swear I just heard someone yelling for help."

V tried to listen, but all she could hear was Laquat yelling at her Grannie Upsha to give her back her amethyst sweater, Elba's high-pitched giggle, and Ha's hollering for Bon to stop running so he could punch him in the face.

"There it is again!" said Instructor Verin.

V strained her ears, but it was no use. All she could hear now was Bon wailing as he tripped over a half-eaten cake and tumbled across the floor, crashing into Kesh's legs.

Laquat, Elba, Ha, and Truj all tripped over the same half-eaten cake and pretty soon there was a massive heap of flailing body parts. Giblit, having narrowly escaped the calamity by leaping out of Bon's arms, had been picked up by Prince Seff and was perched on his shoulder.

Instructor Verin shrugged. "Perhaps I was mistaken." Reaching up, he felt around V's head and pulled a pancake out of her hair. "Don't worry," he said, "there were no pieces of parchment paper or cupcake wrappers involved in making these." The pancake disappeared beneath his bucket.

A split-second later, Rainbow Jon ran into the dining hall, his face ghostly white, his hair sticking out every which way. "Help!" he cried, collapsing to the floor. "It's happened again! We're all doomed!"

Stuarp, who'd become tangled in the heap of flailing body parts, fought his way over to Rainbow Jon. "What's happened again?" he asked, chunks of cake and frosting clinging to his cloud costume. "Why are we all doomed?"

"The Planet Destroyer!" Rainbow Jon gasped. "It's done it again! It's destroyed another planet!"

16

V couldn't sleep, and it wasn't because Instructor Verin was snoring louder than any washing machine could rattle, or because his foot was propped up on her cot, right next to her face, it was because of the Planet Destroyer. After Rainbow Jon's alarming announcement, she and the instructor had rushed up to their room and turned on the telly. Over and over, they'd watched the black, crescent ship move in on the ancient world of Praun and blow it to pieces.

A loud snort came from Instructor Verin and he rolled over, his other foot flopping onto her cot, making it so that both his feet were blissfully resting right next to her face. She tried to push the feet away, but that only made them move closer, one of them touching her cheek. Letting out her own snort—one of annoyance and disgust—she sat up. Why she hadn't thought to move her cot to the other side of the room, she had no idea. Then again, she'd been utterly horrified by what happened to the small, green world; as well as exhausted from running up forty-seven floors.

Her eyes flickered to the instructor, who was completely zonked, and then to the telly. Crawling to the end of her cot, she turned it on. The tiny box sputtered to life and a familiar face greeted her. "Jiji?"

Jiji was in the kitchen, standing on his step stool. He was smiling, but the smile looked uncomfortable on his pinched, crumb smeared face. In each of his hands, was one of Grula's cupcakes,

"V was such a wonderful addition to our kitchen," he was saying. "She is greatly missed."

V was about to roll her eyes, when it occurred to her that maybe he really *was* missing her. After all, who was doing the cleaning, scrubbing, and organizing now? Certainly not... *him*?

Grula was next on the telly. Standing behind two large trays of pinecones (or were they cupcakes?), it was easy to see she was wearing her blue hip waders—the school had flooded again.

"So, Grula," a reporter named Steve was asking, "what do you think of all this?"

Grula glared into the camera. "I want to know how my application got overlooked and how V's got accepted. That girl never baked a day in her—"

The camera cut out and then came back on. It was still pointed at Grula.

"V was such a wonderful addition to our kitchen," the cook said, through clenched teeth. "She is greatly missed."

The camera cut out again, seconds later showing Steve inside Secretary Ophelia's office. The secretary was sitting in her upside-down chair at her upside-down, stuck-in-the-ceiling table, a lion's mane of olive-green flowers hanging from her glasses. Directly beneath her, was the stuffed hippopotamus.

"Tell me," said Steve, "What do you think about two of your school's employees going onto the greatest baking show ever to exist?"

Smirking, Secretary Ophelia pushed the button on her

table. Bzzz! Bzzz! Bzzz!

"Okay... that's not quite the response I was expecting, but perhaps you didn't hear me. Steve cleared his throat, this time shouting, "What do you think about two of your school's employees going onto the greatest baking show ever to exist?"

Secretary Ophelia pushed the button again. Bzzzzzzz!

Steve looked at the camera and drew a hand across his throat, the feed cutting out. When it came back on, he was walking into Headmaster Baz's office.

The headmaster was sitting at his desk, scowling.

"Tell us, Headmaster, how does it feel having so much attention on your lowly school?"

"Don't you mean decrepit school?" he barked, snapping his fingers.

The stuffed hippopotamus suddenly appeared in front of the camera and Steve squealed. The camera cut out and when it came back on the hippopotamus was gone, as was Steve's self-assured attitude.

"So, Headmaster Baz," he said in a quavering voice. "What do you think about V, the girl who once cleaned your school, participating in that Baking Adventures Everyone... Everyone-has-a-good-time...? Show...? Did you know she had such a soul-crushing, socially frowned-upon ailment?"

"I think it was a surprise," said Headmaster Baz. "And I had no idea she suffered from cupcakitosis. Then again, it does explain Grula's constant complaining about missing cupcakes."

"You must be sitting on pins and needles waiting to see the show," Steve replied.

"Surprisingly, yes. Although, I'm not sure you and I are talking about the same show. Now, if you don't mind, I have better things to do than listen to decrepit newsmen…"

The camera feed cut out. Moments later, a woman with magenta hair appeared on the telly.

"Thank you, Steve, for that report. It was so insightful. Now, to our next story: Prince Seff Pip of Rohema, also a competitor in this weeks' B-A-F-T-F-E-A-T-T-C, has particularly close ties to Praun, as his reported fiancé, Autia Noria, Princess of Praun, was known to have been on the planet when it was destroyed. Reporters have been unable to reach the hunky, one-eared prince for questioning, as he's currently preparing for the bake-off tomorrow, but we can be sure that ratings for the popular show will be at an all-time high…"

Prince Seff's fiancé just *died*? V thought. She turned off the telly and flopped back on her cot. Only by then, Instructor Verin's feet had commandeered her pillow. Grumbling, she got up and began pacing the floor, tripping over the instructor's bucket. With an agitated sigh, she grabbed it and clambered to her feet; she couldn't think—not through all the snores—and so went out into the hallway.

"All you have to do is make sure he takes at least one bite," someone was whispering around the corner.

"And then what?" another person replied, something akin to worry in their voice. "Why just one bite?"

"Because…" the other person seemed to hesitate, "…because then, he'll be… *happy*."

Irritated that she couldn't find peace and quiet anywhere, V put the bucket on her head and resumed pacing. Not long after, she bumped into a wall and with a loud clattering thud, crumpled to the ground.

"Ouch!" she moaned, lifting the bucket off her head.

"Worst idea *ever*." Seconds later, a door to the side of her opened.

"V?" said a deep voice.

She looked up and saw Prince Seff staring down at her. Her first instinct was to scream because he was so monstrously huge from down on the floor. But instead, she bit the inside of her cheek.

"What are you doing out here?" he asked. He sounded tired, and his dark eyes were red rimmed as though he'd been crying. "I heard someone fall but I didn't expect it to be you."

"Then who *did* you expect?" she asked, numerous jabs of pain shooting through her body.

Prince Seff shrugged. "I don't know, I've had a number of visitors tonight; Stuarp came by a while ago, as did Mr. Dolop, Rainbow Jon, and Bon to give me their condolences." He scratched his chin. "I'm still trying to figure out why."

V groaned and tried to sit up.

"Here, let me help." Smelling strongly of onions, Prince Seff bent over and gently pulled her to her feet. He then picked up the bucket and handed it to her. "Isn't this your assistant's?"

"Yeah." She rubbed the back of her neck and took the bucket. "Thanks, but, what do you mean you don't know why they gave their condolences? Your fiancé just died."

"Fiancé?" Prince Seff looked puzzled.

"Yeah—the lady on the news said that Autia something, Princess of Praun, was your fiancé."

Prince Seff's lips turned down. "No. I'm not engaged to anyone. And as far as Autia goes, we hated each other. At least, I hated her—she was really mean. One time, she lit my socks on fire *while* I was wearing them."

"That's awful." V shuddered at the thought. "But are you

sure she wasn't your fiancé? The news lady seemed pretty certain. And your eyes…"

"I'm positive, and there's nothing wrong with my eyes. Goodnight, V." A peculiar expression crossing his face, Prince Seff stepped back inside his room and shut the door.

17

V awoke on the floor, the side of her face mashed into the blue shag carpet.

"Sweet dreams?" someone asked.

"What?" She blinked through hazy eyes.

"Were your dreams sweet?"

"Were my dreams sweet?" she repeated in a croaky voice. She blinked again and Instructor Verin came into focus; he was sitting on one of the cots, shining his shoes with a pillowcase—probably because there weren't any towels.

"Yes," he said. "Mine were, in case you were wondering."

"I wasn't, actually…" V realized then that she was clutching his bucket to her chest as though it was really a stuffed animal, or perhaps, a fluffy pillow. Letting go of it, she slowly pushed her stiff, achy body up into a seated position. "… but I'm glad someone got some sleep—I certainly didn't."

Instructor Verin nodded knowingly. "It was that flock of ostriches that flew past our room last night, wasn't it?"

Flock of ostriches? She reached up and touched her forehead; it was tender from running into the wall the night before. "What are you talking about? I couldn't sleep because of your awful snoring, and—"

"A sound which you are undoubtedly mistaking as coming from me," he interjected, "but was *actually* coming from the *ostriches*."

V rolled her eyes. "Ostriches can't fly, and even if they *could*, they wouldn't be snoring and flying at the same time—you're just making up excuses. And it wasn't just your snoring that kept me awake, your feet are pillow-thieving *demons*."

"I still say it was the ostriches. And as far as my feet go, they're partial to pillows." Instructor Verin finished shining his shoes and set the pillowcase on the floor. "How'd they smell?"

"How'd they smell?"

"Yes, one needs to know these things—foul foot odors are amongst the vilest of incivilities."

V scrunched up her nose. "I don't know. A bit flowery, maybe?"

"Good." He smiled, his eyes dropping to the bucket. Within seconds it was floating to him.

A clump of matted, curly hair fell across V's face, and she brushed it aside; now that he wasn't trying to steal a cupcake from her—not that she wanted to eat one ever again—she couldn't help being impressed by his ability. But she wasn't about to tell him that. Instead, she looked around for something else to talk about and saw his yellow book lying beside him on the cot. "Why do you collect those 'Perpetually Unending Story' articles?" she asked.

"You mean this wonderful tale of adventure and mishap?" He reached down and patted the book.

"Yeah, I guess."

"Well, to be honest, I've been trying to decipher its unique combination of creativity and imagination in hopes that it will help me be a better worldmaker."

V's stomach wrenched; the story *did* have creativity and imagination, but it was also unfinished, unending for a reason. "And have you?"

"No, I'm about ninety-five percent there, though. But enough about me, I can be discussed later. A notice was delivered early this morning and it said we're expected in the lobby in exactly...," He checked his watch, "...seventeen minutes."

Seventeen minutes later, a very tired, but showered V stepped into the lobby. Spatula in one hand, she haphazardly smoothed her pink, cupcake dress with the other hand before fiddling with her wet hair.

"Stop fidgeting, Vivi," Instructor Verin whispered from inside his bucket. "You look fine."

"No, I don't," she hissed. "I've never looked fine a single day in my life, and now I'm about to be on a show where everyone in the galaxy will see me." The reality of it hadn't hit her until she was halfway down the stairs, mostly because her mind had been so busy thinking about other things, but also because she'd never cared much about her appearance—she'd never had to. But now, everyone would see her frizzy hair and whatever awkward mannerisms she'd adopted from growing up alone in the basement of a ramshackle school for worldmakers. And her anxiety over the instructor's deciphering of the 'Perpetually Unending Story' articles wasn't helping matters. "But you wouldn't know anything about how I feel, because you *always* look fine."

"Oh, really? Well, I don't suppose you've forgotten who you're talking to? Nobody ever looked at Ooblick the way people look at you."

"Yeah, because he was so much better looking than me." She knew that wasn't at all true, but at the moment, it had seemed an appropriate thing to say.

With a loud snort, Instructor Verin burst out laughing and

laughed so hard, and for so long, that he had to excuse himself to find a toilet.

Scowling, V surveyed the lobby. Most of the other competitors were standing near Stuarp—who was once again a pristinely white cloud—and were participating in another round of his calming stretches.

"Good morning!" said a deep, cheerful voice.

V looked up and saw Prince Seff smiling down at her. His eyes were no longer red-rimmed, nor did he look tired. "Oh. It's you," she said flatly.

He raised an eyebrow. "Rough morning?"

"You could say that." She used her spatula to swat a strand of hair from her face.

"Well, I just came over to apologize for my behavior last night."

"Apologize?" She swatted at her hair again. "Why?"

"Because I didn't realize until I saw my reflection in the bathroom mirror that it looked as though I'd been crying. Which would make perfect sense had I just lost a fiancé, but the truth is, I was eating an onion." He pulled an onion out of the pouch on his belt and took a bite, his eyes getting all red and watery. "Delicious, but quite potent."

V tried not to think about how bad his breath was going to smell. "If Autia wasn't your fiancé, then why are the news people saying she was?"

"Propaganda. It doesn't matter if a story is true or not, it only matters if it will catch someone's attention. Mind you, there were several attempts made by both her people and mine to get us together, but she was far too ferocious for my taste."

"What do you mean?" V asked, her curiosity outweighing her irritation with Instructor Verin.

"Well, after the sock-burning incident, I tried to get her to see a psychiatrist, but she absolutely refused and threw a statue of a watermelon at my head."

"Oh, I see your point."

Prince Seff smiled sadly before looking at the other side of the lobby where Elba was tugging on one of Kesh's arms with both hands and climbing up one of his legs with both feet. "What happened to your nose?" the little girl was asking him in a loud, taunting voice. "Did it get bitten off? Or were you born without it?"

"I suppose I'd best be off to rescue my friend, again," Prince Seff said, taking another bite of onion. "I'll see you later, V. Good luck in the teepee."

As he strode off, Instructor Verin clunked into the lobby. He had a single bucket stuck on one foot, and two buckets stacked together stuck on his other foot.

"I take it you had trouble finding the toilet?" V said when he stopped beside her. She was still upset with him for laughing at her; he of all people should know that being ugly and awkward wasn't funny.

"I did, indeed; I must say that my goal to avoid buckets isn't going so well. But this bucket..." he tapped the bucket on his head, "... has been a lifesaver."

"So where'd you get the other buckets?" she asked irritably.

"A closet, I think. And being in there gave me a few minutes of really good thinking time."

"Oh really? What'd you think about?"

"Who the headmaster's application was for. And even though I'm not one hundred percent on this, I'm fairly certain Prince Seff and Kesh are our guys."

V glared at the bucket on Instructor Verin's head; isn't that what she'd suggested to him the day before and he'd completely shut her down? "And why do you say that?"

"Because of what you said yesterday: you asked when the last time was that I'd seen two people as tall as the ones exiting the hover-bus. I didn't think about it at the time because I was too distraught about not having more mirrors, a shoe tree, and any furniture. But, in hindsight, I believe you made an excellent point: Rohems are the tallest race of humankind in the galaxy; the odds of getting two men that tall from anywhere else are astronomical."

"Okay, so you now think the application was for Prince Seff and Kesh, but do you also think they were the two men we saw with Headmaster Baz?"

"I don't know. But that's your next mission—to find out."

Suddenly, a banshee-like wail ricocheted through the lobby; Prince Seff was dangling Elba upside down by her feet again.

"Put me down you oversized giraffe!" the little girl screeched. "I'll tell my mom!"

Prince Seff laughed.

Kesh glowered.

The other competitors showed signs of agitation.

"Everyone stay calm," Stuarp said.

But a second later, Laquat whopped Stuarp on the shins with her cane, Truj ran to a potted plant and started throwing handfuls of dirt into the air, and Ha punched a hole in the wall.

Oh no, V thought, with a groan. Not again… Without a second thought—there was no way she was going through a rerun of the night before—she took off running for the front doors. Halfway there, she heard a thunk and then an "Ouch!"

and then what sounded like several buckets clanking together. Glancing over her shoulder, she saw Instructor Verin lying in a crumpled heap on the floor. Hurriedly, she swerved back to him, pulled him to his feet and dragged him outside into the courtyard where they came face to face—or in the instructor's case, bucket to face—with a bot holding a firehose. V quickly moved out of the way and the bot tromped into the Blue Sparkle. The sounds of spraying water and screaming immediately followed. Seemingly unaware of what was happening, Instructor Verin gravitated towards the street where hordes of women were pressed up against a short, white fence, screaming his name and frantically waving their arms in the air to get his attention. How they knew it was him inside the bucket, V had no idea, but she wasn't going to hang around and find out. Tightening her grip on his arm, she hurried to the teepee. But it wasn't easy with him lopsidedly clunking beside her, flapping his arms and bowing at what he likely thought were adoring fans, but was actually a row of outhouses.

"Hey!" someone called. "Wait up!"

V slowed herself and the instructor to a stop as a man with spiky, red hair jogged up to them.

"Name's Cannon," he said, grinning from ear to ear. "I just want you to know how much I admired your demonstration yesterday. Selling cupcake fertilizer isn't easy as most people want to *eat* cupcakes. But after seeing you spit yours out the way you did... well, I think people are going to change their minds."

"I wasn't demonstrating anything," said V.

"It's true," Instructor Verin chimed in. "The reason she spat it out was because Palfrey Dolop makes cupcake wrappers and parchment paper out of recycled toilet paper."

Cannon's ear to ear grin widened. "You're serious, aren't you?" he said, looking at Instructor Verin's bucket and then at V. "He's serious, isn't he?"

V nodded.

"Wow!" He ran a hand over his spiky hair and looked around.

At the same time, the spraying water in the lobby shut off.

"Well, that's my cue to go," he said, before sprinting away.

"Who was that?" Instructor Verin asked.

"Just some nutter," V said, tugging him inside the teepee.

The other competitors weren't far behind, all of them soaked. Only Stuarp was smiling.

"I feel just like a rain cloud," he said, wringing the water out of his cloud costume.

Bon limped in a minute or so later, a white bandage wrapped around his head and a look of intense fear in his eyes. Huffing and puffing behind him, microphone and black box in his arms, was Rainbow Jon.

Bon took the microphone from Rainbow Jon and turned it on. "Please find your baking station," he said in a trembling voice. "It has your name on it." He gestured to eight individual countertops circling the inside of the teepee. Each had its own set of shelves and cabinets, and each was a different color of the rainbow.

Following some confusion as Ha didn't know how to read and Laquat kept thinking everyone else's baking stations were hers, all the bakers were soon seated on turned-over trash bins at their assigned baking stations.

Seated at the baking station to one side of V was Ha. Seated at the baking station to the other side of her was Prince

Seff. Seated on the turned-over trash bin right beside her was Instructor Verin.

"Do you mind getting these off?" he asked from inside his bucket. He held up one of his bucketed feet.

Letting out an agitated huff, V leaned over, tugging on the single bucket. At the same time, Bon resumed speaking,

"Mr. Dolop sends his regrets at not being here for the introduction to the first bake but would like to assure you that he will be here for the judging. So...," he sucked in a very shaky breath, "...in his absence, and at his request, I will go over the rules..."

"It's odd that Palfrey's not doing the introduction," Instructor Verin whispered. "Don't you think, Vivi?"

"Yeah."

"... First rule," continued Bon. "Is that no matter how awful your food might taste, it absolutely has to *look* good. Mr. Dolop will do his best to pretend it *tastes* good..."

After a few more good tugs, the single bucket came off and V got to work on the two stacked-together buckets.

"...Second rule is that you must present *something* to Mr. Dolop. Any questions?"

"Yes," said Stuarp. "Do we have to wear aprons?"

"We actually don't have aprons right now, due to the remodel," said Bon. "And if you haven't already noticed, we don't have stools, either."

Struggling to remove the buckets, V knelt on the floor for more leverage.

"Oh good," replied Stuarp. "Clouds don't wear aprons *or* sit on stools, so I don't either. "

Just then, V gave an extra hard tug, and the buckets flew off Instructor Verin's foot, soaring clear over her head and into the center of the teepee.

Thunk! Thud! *Squeeaaaakkkkk*!

She froze, her eyes on Instructor Verin. Peeking out from under his bucket, his focus was somewhere beyond the baking station. He motioned for V to get on her trash bin. She did so, following his gaze to where Bon lay unconscious. *Oh no,* she thought, trying to make herself as small as possible. And yet, the other competitors hadn't seemed to notice what she'd done; Laquat was curled up on her baking station, fast asleep; Ha was trying to stick his fingers into a set of beaters while turning them on; Truj was squirting mustard on the teepee wall behind him or her; Elba was blowing a mouthful of gum into a bubble larger than her head; Prince Seff was eating an onion; and Kesh was staring at V, an uncomfortable, longing look on his nose-less face.

A shudder ran through her and she quickly returned her attention to the center of the teepee where Stuarp and Rainbow Jon were trying to revive Bon, but without success.

Eventually, Rainbow Jon stood up. "So… I guess I'll be the one giving you your assignment: bake one sandwich. It has to have mustard, lettuce, and bacon on it, but you can put other toppings on it too. Supplies are on the shelves inside your baking stations and in the storeroom." He pointed to a door-shaped flap of white fabric at the back of the teepee. "You have one hour, so get started."

18

"One hour to make a sandwich?" asked V.

"Bake," Instructor Verin corrected. "One hour to *bake* a sandwich."

"Bake? Oh, yeah, bake; I've never baked a sandwich before, I've *made* one—several, actually—but I already had the bread." By then, the majority of V's bad mood was gone; knocking Bon unconscious had made her realize that all she'd been doing that morning was pitying herself.

"I'm sure you'll figure something out," Instructor Verin said, running a comb down the side of his bucket. "In the meantime, I'm going to speak with the other competitors just to make absolutely sure none of them got Headmaster Baz's application. And that we're correct in our assumption it went to Prince Seff and Kesh."

"You're doing that right now? But you're supposed to be assisting me; I can't bake, remember?"

"Neither can I, but we're looking at the bigger picture here. Besides, how hard can it be to make a sandwich?"

"Bake," V corrected.

"Yes, how hard can it be to bake a sandwich?"

"Really hard—I don't know how to make bread."

"You'll be fine, just do what the other competitors are doing."

"Maybe you haven't noticed," she said, lowering her

voice, "but the other competitors are *crazy*."

"Precisely. You're going to be fine."

"But someone's bound to notice you're not assisting me."

"And just who might that be?"

"Well…" V glanced around; Laquat was still sleeping, Elba was blowing more bubbles, Ha was still playing daredevil with the beaters, Truj was still squirting mustard everywhere, Stuarp was enthusiastically weaving pieces of paper together, and Prince Seff and Kesh were leaving the teepee.

"Believe me," Instructor Verin went on, "None of these wackadoodles is going to notice, and if any of them manage to make a real loaf of bread, I'll eat my shoes for dinner." Peeking out from under his bucket, he got to his feet and walked over to Ha.

Shaking her head and hoping he was right, V knelt down beside her baking station. On the top shelf was a stack of construction paper, a pair of scissors, a roll of tape, a bottle of glue, and some glitter. On the bottom shelf was a bottle of mustard, a bottle of catsup, a jar of mayonnaise, and a jar of cocoa powder. She searched the oven and proving drawer next. They were empty. The storeroom wasn't much better; aside from several containers of colored playdough, the shelves were bare. Wondering what in the worlds was going on, she took some of the playdough and returned to her baking station.

Unsteadily swaying from side to side, a barely conscious Bon was waiting for her with a tray of six cupcakes. All of the wrappers had been removed. "They're fresh out of the oven," he said before teetering off.

Stomach churning, V contemplated dumping the cupcakes into the trash until she noticed Prince Seff giving her an encouraging thumbs up. Trying to look happy, she scooped a bit of frosting off the top of the nearest cupcake and forced it into her mouth.

Prince Seff smiled and looked away.

V glanced around to make sure no one else was watching before pushing the tray of cupcakes aside. She then got to work puzzling out how to make a sandwich without any sandwich ingredients. Midway into flattening a piece of white playdough into what would hopefully look like a real slice of bread, two fists thumped down on her countertop.

"What makes you so special that you get cupcakes and the rest of us don't?" Ha roared. Behind him, Rainbow Jon was hurrying over, a ginormous and ancient model of camcorder on his shoulder.

V quickly looked around for Instructor Verin and found him speaking with Elba, his voice echoing loudly out of the bucket on his head. Clearly, she was on her own. "Because I need them for my cupcakitosis."

"Ha!" yelled Ha. "If that's true then why did the news people say you had *chocolatetruffletosis*?"

"Chocolatetruffletosis?" Her eyes flickered back to Instructor Verin, who was still speaking.

"Yes!" said Ha. "And if you don't eat chocolate truffles, you start twirling in circles like a ballerina!"

"No, I'm pretty sure it's cupcakes I have to eat."

Ha thumped his fists on the countertop a second time. "Then why didn't Mr. Dolop say anything about it at the briefing?"

"I don't know."

"You don't know, do you? We'll see about that!" Ha picked up a cupcake.

Rainbow Jon and the camcorder moved in even closer.

V suddenly realized that if she was going to keep up her charade, she needed to step up her game—it was time for some action. Silently, she cleared her throat and sucked in a huge breath of air, "PUT THAT CUPCAKE DOWN YOU UGLY RHINOCEROS! AND GO AWAY BEFORE I RIP YOUR FINGERNAILS OFF!"

That seemed to do the trick because Ha froze and then ever so slowly put the cupcake down before running back to his baking station.

Satisfied with her performance, V was about to resume "bread making" when she noticed Bon and Rainbow Jon watching her expectantly. Only, she wasn't sure what they were expecting—more yelling perhaps? More drama to show on the telly? She could see the headlines now: 'Cupcakatosis Victim Ruthlessly Yells at Fellow Bakers While Making a Sandwich.' "AND THAT GOES FOR THE REST OF YOU TOO!" she shouted, shaking her spatula at the other competitors.

Bon nodded approvingly and Rainbow Jon trained the aged camcorder on someone else.

V resumed molding her slice of bread.

Moments later, Prince Seff walked over. "Would you mind sharing some of your red playdough?" he asked.

"Sure." She handed him the container. "Isn't it strange that we're baking with playdough and paper and glue?"

"Yes, but I can't say anything about it because my whole reason for being here is to promote peace."

"I suppose that does complicate things," she agreed.

Prince Seff nodded and turned to leave, but then stopped, a concerned expression crossing his face. "Perhaps you should eat some of your cupcakes? I can tell you've been feeling a little on edge."

In an effort to be convincing, V reached for a cupcake, but then pulled her hand back at the last second. "I can't," she quietly admitted. "I wish I could, but I found out yesterday that the cupcake wrappers on Fooda are made of recycled toilet paper."

"Really?" Prince Seff's face paled.

"Yeah."

"I'm not sure what to tell you," he said. "I wish I did, but I don't."

"It's okay. I'll just keep eating the frosting. Hopefully, that will be enough for now."

The prince smiled sympathetically and left.

V spent the remainder of her time designing and creating what she felt was the perfect model for a real sandwich: two slices of white playdough bread, a large red playdough tomato, three pieces of green playdough lettuce, five strips of brown and tan playdough bacon, mustard (which had turned out to be yellow paint), and mayonnaise (which had turned out to be white paint).

"How's your sandwich coming along, Vivi?" Instructor Verin asked, walking up beside her.

"I'm done," she replied. "There was no real food to bake with, so I had to use playdough."

"Hmmm... This is all getting very suspicious, isn't it? A baking show with no real baking?"

"Yeah, but I'm okay with it."

"Good, because I believe it's the miracle we've been hoping for." Unable to see because of his bucket, Instructor Verin clapped a hand on top of V's head.

"Yeah, I guess you're right," she said, moving his hand

down to her shoulder. "So, what did you find out?"

"About what?"

"The other competitors."

"Oh, right, about that—it's quite the story. Are you sure you want to hear it?"

"Of course, I do."

"Okay, but you're only getting the condensed version." He cleared his throat. "Ha has an evil twin sister who breeds grumpy pigmy Chihuahuas; Elba's ultimate dream is to become the first person to swim through molten lava and live; Laquat insists she has forty-two biological children made out of diamonds, only she can't remember what happened to them; Truj wrote a self-help book on how all flowers are really deceased gods from other galaxies; and Stuarp is raising money to feed starving clouds."

"Wow. I can't imagine what the full version must have been like."

"You have *no* idea. And after all that, I'm still unclear on where they got their applications." Instructor Verin sighed heavily. "On a lighter note, how are you? Any luck with…?" he pointed a finger at Truj.

"Why would I need luck with Truj?"

"No, not Truj." He pointed again, this time at Elba.

"Elba?"

"*No.*" Instructor Verin continued to point at the other competitors, eventually getting to Prince Seff.

"*Ohhh.*" V finally understood what he was asking her: if she'd questioned the prince about being at the school with Headmaster Baz. "No. Not yet."

Just then, Bon limped into the center of the teepee. "Time! Everyone, step away from your sandwiches! Rainbow Jon has gone to fetch Mr. Dolop so sit tight until he arrives!"

V sat down on her trash bin.

Instructor Verin sat too, and missed his trash bin, crashing to the floor. But after another go at it, was safely seated. "Is someone screaming?" he asked.

A second later, a screaming Rainbow Jon ran into the teepee. "Aaaaahhhhhhhhh! It's struck again! The Planet Destroyer has struck again! Dort is gone!"

19

"Give me a cupcake," demanded a gruff voice.

Startled, V looked up; she wasn't sure how long she'd been sitting on her trash bin for, just staring at the floor, but it couldn't have been more than a few minutes. "Come again?"

A teary-eyed Ha pointed to the tray of cupcakes on her baking station.

"Oh…" Realizing what he wanted, she picked one up and handed it to him. Under normal circumstances, she probably would have yelled again, and might have even thrown something, but, another planet being destroyed was *not* normal. At least, it wasn't *supposed* to be normal.

"Er…thanks," Ha grumbled under his breath.

No sooner had he shuffled off, than Elba, Laquat, and Truj bustled over, each insisting on having their own cupcakes, *too*.

V handed over the entire tray.

If Bon noticed, he didn't say anything. He just limped around in circles, Giblit clutched to his chest.

Suddenly, Rainbow Jon collapsed to the floor in a sobbing heap.

"There, there, now, it's okay," Stuarp said, rushing over to him.

Meanwhile, Prince Seff was at his baking station with Kesh,

"I need more green playdough," Kesh was saying. "I ran

out."

"Then, go get some," said the prince.

"No. You have some—give me yours."

"No."

"Yes."

"No."

"I'm older, and that means you have to do what I say," Kesh said.

"No, it doesn't," said Prince Seff.

"Yes, it does."

"No, it doesn't. I'm a *prince,* so *you* have to do what *I* say…"

"What do you think about all this?" V asked, turning to Instructor Verin.

Seated on his turned-over trash bin, he ran a comb down the side of his bucket. "It's terrible. Not only are the Planet Destroyer's attacks becoming more frequent, but it's destroying the oldest worlds with the most irreplaceable histories."

"It is?"

"Yes. Dort with its ancient libraries, Praun with its rare life forms, Hulse with—"

V nudged him in the ribs. "Palfrey's here."

He quickly put the comb away and straightened his bucket. "Do you notice anything suspicious about Mr. Too-hot-to-trot-Dolop?"

She pursed her lips; Palfrey's arms hung down at his sides, his clothes were freshly pressed, his hair neatly combed, and he wore a downcast expression.

"No."

"Drats—I was really hoping you would."

"Hello, everyone," Palfrey said, picking up the microphone. "I know that the most terrible news has befallen us today, especially considering how only last night, Praun was also destroyed. However, we will not give in to such tyranny. We will compose ourselves and get ready for the judging."

A sniffling Rainbow Jon got to his feet and propped the camcorder on his shoulder. Bon, with Giblit perched on the top of his head, pushed an empty dishwasher box into the center of the teepee.

Palfrey walked up to the box. "Laquat!"

The old woman instantly woke up from her latest nap—which had begun a few minutes before—and hobbled up to Palfrey, handing him one of her glittery purple shoes. She then turned to leave but was stopped by Bon.

"You have to stay at the box while Palfrey judges your bake," he explained, nervously wringing his hands.

"No one tells me what to do!" Laquat squawked. Wielding her cane, she walloped Bon in the stomach and hobbled off.

With a cry of pain, he collapsed to the floor, a disgruntled Giblit leaping off his head.

Seeming to not notice, Palfrey stared at the shoe. "Ah, a shoe sandwich. Such a delicious treat, wouldn't you agree Bon?"

Curled up in a ball, Bon painfully gasped, "Yes, yes, very... delicious."

Palfrey tried to cut the shoe with a pocketknife, but it didn't cut. So, he picked it up and pretended to take a bite out of it like one would a cob of corn. "Presentation's good, but the texture is too tight—a bit stodgy. What do you think, Bon?"

Bon slowly dragged himself to the box, took the shoe, and also pretended to take a bite. "I quite like it," he said between gasps. "I don't mind the tight... texture. It reminds me of summer with all of the... glitter. It's definitely something I... would both wear and eat that time of... year."

"Great. Thank you, Bon. And you too, Laquat. Well done." Palfrey's eyes scanned the teepee, coming to rest on the old woman who was taking another nap on her baking station. "Let's have Elba up here next."

Hopping to her feet, the little girl skipped up to the dishwasher box and handed Palfrey her tray. On it, was a sock stuffed with a massive wad of blue gum.

Palfrey smiled, but it looked forced. "What a delicious treat of a sandwich you've made, Elba. I don't even have to taste it to know it's good. Wouldn't you say so, Bon?"

Back on his feet, Bon grimaced. "Yes."

"Really?" Elba squeaked. "Does this mean I'm going to the next round?"

"Yes." Palfrey said, his smile starting to crack. "It does."

"Yes! Yes! Yes! Yes! Yes!" Elba grabbed her tray and skipped back to her baking station.

"Truj?" called Palfrey.

Visibly caught off-guard, a wide-eyed Truj slowly plodded up to the dishwasher box with a half-eaten cupcake.

Palfrey looked down at the cupcake and then up at Truj. "Very good," he said. "You may go back to your seat. Stuarp!"

Smiling brightly, Stuarp carried a handwoven paper basket up to the dishwasher box. Inside the basket was a handwoven sandwich filled with handwoven condiments.

Palfrey took a nibble of the sandwich before telling Stuarp that his bread was under-proved and underdone. "But not doughy, it just needed more time in the oven. Ha!"

No longer teary-eyed, Ha marched up to Palfrey and gave

him a one-hundred-dollar bill. "That's a money sandwich!" he barked. "Don't spend it all in one place!"

Prince Seff was next with a sandwich made of playdough.

"This sandwich certainly looks delicious," said Palfrey, picking it up and taking a bite. Both cheeks puffed up and a convulsion ran through his body. A painful looking swallow ensued. "Very nice," he said in a tight, gravelly voice. "Texture's good, excellent flavor, and excellent bake. Couldn't have been better." He handed the sandwich to Bon.

After taking a bite, Bon ran out of the teepee and vomited. Upon his return, he rasped, "Not my favorite flavor, but the bake is excellent."

"Thank you," said Prince Seff.

"Kesh!"

With a grunt, Kesh stood up, a piece of paper in his hands. Striding up to the dishwasher box, he set it down in front of Palfrey.

Wondering what had happened to the all the green playdough he'd been kneading, V craned her neck to see what was on the paper. From what she could tell, it was a *drawing* of a sandwich.

"It does look a bit under-proved," Palfrey said. "But overall, a delicious looking sandwich."

Kesh nodded and said a gruff, "Thank you."

"And last, but not least, we have V."

Heart suddenly pounding, V stood up.

"You can do this!" Instructor Verin whispered.

Hoping he was right, V made her way to the dishwasher box and set down her playdough sandwich.

Briefly, Palfrey glanced at it before asking Bon to fetch a magnifying glass.

"Certainly," he said, limping away.

Turning to V, Palfrey leaned across the dishwasher box and smiled. Not a cracked, plastic smile like the one he'd worn for Elba. This was a smile that made his white teeth sparkle. "So," he whispered. "I need to know—are you and that assistant of yours together? Not as in you came on the show together—of course you did—but are you *together,* together?"

Together, together? V's brow furrowed in confusion; what other kind of together would she and Instructor Verin be? It dawned on her then, what Palfrey meant, and her cheeks flushed with heat. "No."

"Wonderful news!" Palfrey said. "Maybe we can—"

Just then, Bon returned with the magnifying glass, handing it to Palfrey.

"Ah, yes, thank you, Bon." Palfrey winked at V before picking up the playdough sandwich and examining every inch of it. "It looks as though you've outdone yourself; great presentation, great texture, and absolutely great smell, which we all know means great taste." He set down the sandwich and magnifying glass, taking V's hand in his, shaking it for a good thirty seconds. "Yes, very well done. I will have to get the recipe for this one. Later, perhaps?"

Cheeks burning, V replied, "Okay." As soon as he let go of her hand, she picked up her sandwich and hurried back to her seat. Along the way, she spotted an enraged scowl on Kesh's face. It was aimed directly at Palfrey.

"I will now reveal the person who will be dismissed from the show," Palfrey announced. "That person is… *Waffer*!"

Ha, Truj, Elba, and Laquat cheered. Stuarp burst into tears but was smiling. Prince Seff clapped. Kesh's scowl deepened.

"Who's Waffer?" V wondered aloud.

"The bot will be in momentarily to retrieve Waffer," he continued. "In the meantime, try to relax. Your next bake starts in ten minutes, and you will be making a wedding cake. Three tiers, cream fillings, lots of decoration—it must be absolutely gorgeous! And when the clock starts you will have exactly twenty minutes!"

V tapped on Instructor Venn's bucket. "Did you hear that?" she whispered. "Palfrey just dismissed a competitor who doesn't exist."

"Yes," he whispered back. "Very peculiar."

Moments later, a bot entered the teepee. In its arms was a huge tray of assorted cakes which it began handing out to the competitors. For the most part, no one objected to what they were given... except for Ha.

"I insist that you give me that slice of lemon-strawberry cake on the tray!" he shouted when the bot handed him a slice of orange cake. The bot bonked him on the head with a metal fist and gave him the orange cake anyway.

When the bot got to V, it handed her two slices of apple cake—one for her and one for her assistant.

"You better give those to me," said Instructor Verin. "They might have been baked with parchment paper."

V gave him the cakes and he quickly dropped them into the proving drawer, slamming it shut. Relieved, she looked up just in time to see Prince Seff being handed the coveted piece of lemon-strawberry cake. But something was poking out from between one of the layers. Squinting, she leaned closer for a better look: it was a piece of parchment paper!

"Prince Seff! Don't eat that!" she cried. Jumping to her feet, she ran over and took the plate from his hands.

Prince Seff looked surprised. "Is everything okay, V? If

you like lemon-strawberry cake, I would be more than happy to trade for your apple cake."

"No, it's not *that*." She lowered her voice. "Parchment paper is probably made of recycled toilet paper, *too*."

"Really?" Prince Seff's eyes widened.

"Yes," she said, dropping the cake into the trash.

An abrupt, joyful, *"Whoop!"* sounded in the teepee. Seconds later, Ha ran over to Prince Seff's baking station, scooped the lemon-strawberry cake out of the trash, and ran away, laughing.

20

All V wanted was food that didn't have anything to do with toilet paper, but there didn't seem to be any of that around. Stomach growling, she looked down at her baking station and tried to think of ways to make a three-tiered wedding cake out of nothing but playdough, glue, and glitter

"You have two minutes left!" Bon announced.

V sighed dejectedly. She knew she had to get to work, but she was so tired and so hungry and so... *sluggish*. The feeling had hit her suddenly, just before the bake began, and it was making it really hard to concentrate.

Just then, Instructor Verin returned from a trip to the outhouses. "No extra buckets, V!" he announced proudly from inside his bucket. There was, however, a long ribbon of toilet paper attached to the bottom of his shoe.

Not wanting to ruin his proud moment, she waited until he sat down before quietly removing the toilet paper and setting it on her baking station.

Moments later, Bon announced that the twenty minutes were up, after which, Palfrey strode into the teepee.

"Let's see those wedding cakes," he said.

Laquat was called up to the dishwasher box first, offering her false teeth as her "wedding cake." Stuarp was next with a beautifully woven three-tiered glittery, white, paper cake. Elba had one of Laquat's shoes, inside of which was a huge wad of blue gum. Truj presented his or her empty cake plate and fork.

Prince Seff offered a piece of red construction paper, and Kesh presented a lumpy ball of playdough.

Upon hearing her name called, V grabbed the ribbon of toilet paper. It wasn't the best choice for her bake, but it was better than nothing. Briefly, Palfrey looked it over, and to her immense relief, there were no uncomfortable questions or awkwardly long handshakes. In fact, he hardly noticed her.

"Very good," he said, "You may return to your seat. Ha!"

Ha, who'd fallen asleep at his baking station, didn't stir.

"Ha!" He called again.

When the short, plump, man still didn't stir, Palfrey ordered Bon to go get him.

Looking terrified, Bon limped over and from a few feet away, poked Ha in the shoulder.

No response.

Bon poked him a little harder and when that did nothing, slapped him on the backside of the head. A look of satisfaction crossed his face, but abruptly vanished as Ha fell to the floor. Dried white foam covered his mouth and chin, his glassy eyes staring blankly up at the ceiling.

Bon screamed and then fainted.

Stuarp ran over, Rainbow Jon and the camcorder right behind him. Putting a few fingers on Ha's throat, he shook his head. "He's dead. I can't believe it—he's *dead*!"

21

"Who's dead?" Elba asked, blowing a big, blue bubble. "Bon?"

"No, you stupid girl!" Palfrey snapped. "Ha!"

Elba's face turned purplish red. Her lips and chin quivered and suddenly she was screaming at the top of her lungs, "I am not a stupid girl! You're stupid! You're nothing but a stupid worldmaker who probably doesn't wash his underwear! I hate—"

"Will someone *please* take care of that wretched child?" Palfrey demanded as he knelt down beside Ha.

Prince Seff walked over and grabbed Elba by the ankles, carrying her upside down from the teepee.

Instructor Verin, peeking out from under his bucket, stepped over to Palfrey, who was examining Ha's eyes and mouth.

"He's been—"

"Poisoned," Instructor Verin said, finishing the worldmaker's sentence.

The next few minutes went by in a blur as a bot was summoned to get the body.

Stuarp, whose face had gone as white as his cloud costume, approached Palfrey. "I suppose we should all go back to our rooms, then? This is such a travesty…"

"No. The show must go on; I had to eliminate someone

anyway, so with Ha out, we will continue on to the next round, which will of course, be dedicated to him."

"But—" Stuarp began.

"No buts," said Palfrey. "Continuing this competition is the best way to celebrate Ha's life."

Stuarp didn't seem so sure, but didn't object, going back to his baking station and sitting down.

"Your next bake will be anything of your choice," Palfrey told the competitors. "Your time starts now, and you'll have as long as it takes for me to contact Ha's family and inform them of the bad news."

Stunned, V sat down on her trash bin. How was she supposed to bake anything after what had just happened? What had happened to the planets was horrible too, but she hadn't been there to witness it with her own eyes. Ha might have only been one person, and an angry bully of a person at that, but it was still awful that he'd died, and that she'd seen his dead body.

"Awful, isn't it, Vivi?" Instructor Verin asked, sitting down beside her.

"Yeah."

Silence settled over both of them as Ha's body was wheeled out of the teepee on a metal food cart.

"Do you really think it was poison?" V asked. "Couldn't he have choked on something?"

"No," said Instructor Verin. "If he'd choked, his skin would've had a blue tint to it from lack of oxygen, but it didn't. And he didn't move around at all—if I'd been choking, I'd have done everything I could to get someone's attention."

As alarming as it was to think about, V knew he was right. "What do you think could've poisoned him?"

"Well, we've all been in the teepee all morning, and considering how Ha was fine half-an-hour ago, but is dead now, I'd say whatever poisoned him was fast-acting; it must have been in the cakes the bot brought in."

"But there were all different kinds, and everyone who ate one is doing fine... I think..." V's eyes went to the napping Laquat and for a moment there, she was ready to run to the old lady's side thinking that perhaps, she was dead, also. But then Laquat started talking in her sleep, demanding that someone named Lolu give her back her onyx sweater.

"In that case," said Instructor Verin, "We'll just have to figure out which cake had the poison."

V thought for a moment. "Ha did snatch Prince Seff's lemon-strawberry cake out of the..." Her voice tapered off as she realized what must have happened.

"Out of the what?"

Grabbing Instructor Verin's arm, she pulled him outside, into the nearest outhouse.

"Do we really have to talk in here?" he objected. "It's so smelly. Closets really are a better way to go."

"But there aren't any closets nearby."

"Even better."

"What do you mean, even bet—?"

Instructor Verin pulled V out of the outhouse and into the Blue Sparkle. Soon, they were standing inside a dark closet.

"Ah, the scent of dry cement," he said. "Now please, Vivi, continue on with what you wanted to tell me."

"Right." She inhaled and exhaled. "I think I know what happened: that cake—the lemon-strawberry one—was meant for Prince Seff and had I not taken it from him, he would have eaten it. I think *he* was the one who was supposed to die." As she said it, the conversation she'd overheard the night before came to mind,

"All you have to do is make sure he takes at least one bite."

"And then what? Why just one bite?"

"Because... then, he'll be... happy..."

She quickly told Instructor Verin about it.

"Are you certain?" he asked. "That's a hefty accusation, especially considering they used the word 'happy'."

"I know how it sounds, but it was the way they said it: *happy*. I didn't put any thought into it at the time, but looking back, it's almost like there was a double meaning, like it was some sort of code word."

"It's possible," the instructor mused. "But isn't it also possible they were talking about something else entirely and that the poison being in the cake was an accident?"

"I..." V paused. Could it really have been an accident? "I guess so, but is that what you think happened?"

"No, but we have to explore all possibilities."

"Okay. So, say it was an accident, then what?"

"Then Prince Seff was lucky and Ha was unlucky."

"And if it wasn't an accident?"

"Then you're probably right about someone trying to kill Prince Seff."

"But why would someone want to do that?"

"It could be anything. For one, he's a prince; there's always loads of personal and political unrest when it comes to bureaucracies. And that's not taking into account everything that's going on: he's at odds with his father, the planet's at war... That's more than enough reasons for someone to want him dead."

"But who here would want him dead? And does this have anything to do with Threka? Or Headmaster Baz and the two men at the school?

"I don't know, but that's why you really, really, *really* need to pull the prince aside and speak with him."

"I know, I just haven't had time."

"Then *make* time. And while you're at it, ask him about his bodyguard. Not only does he have the closest ties to him, and therefore a possible motive, but I don't like the kooky way he keeps looking at you. Now, let's get back to the teepee before Palfrey returns."

A few minutes later, V was back at her baking station. Again faced with the perplexing question of what to bake, she reached inside one of the shelves and grabbed the first thing her fingers touched: a bottle of glitter.

"What are you going to make with that?" Instructor Verin asked curiously. Head tilted back; he was looking at her from underneath his bucket.

"Nothing. This is my bake."

"*That* is your bake?"

"Yeah—if you'd seen what the others have been offering up as bakes, this would seem like candy to you."

"Perhaps I'll take my bucket off this round, then; I am rather curious to see what goes on. That and…" he lowered his voice, "… I should keep an eye on Palfrey. After all, Ha's death did occur in *his* teepee and with *his* cakes."

"What about Stuarp?"

"I just won't look at him." A determined expression crossing his face, Instructor Verin took off his bucket and set it on the floor.

Just then, Palfrey walked into the teepee. His once nice,

neat hair was disheveled and his shirt was only halfway tucked in. He also appeared agitated.

"You think Palfrey had something to do with the poisoning?" V whispered. "I thought you said Kesh had the most motive?"

"I said he was the closest to the prince and *could* have a motive, but I'm not ruling anyone out until we know for sure."

A visibly frazzled Bon approached Palfrey. "Shall we get started?"

He nodded.

"Then the time is now yours," said Bon, "unless of course…"

"No, it's fine." Palfrey dismissively waved a hand to the side before calling the competitors up to the dishwasher box.

Elba, who'd seemed to have gotten over her earlier run-in with him, presented a spoon holding a wad of gum. Stuarp had a handwoven cup filled with handwoven hot chocolate,

"To ease the aching soul," he said tearfully.

Laquat gave Palfrey a handful of brittle, yellowed fingernail clippings; Truj put his or her finger into his or her ear and pulled out some earwax; Prince Seff had a bottle of playdough; Kesh had a large dagger; and V handed over the bottle of glitter.

Palfrey didn't say a word during the judging other than to tell everyone to get back to their seats. He then told them they'd all passed and quickly excused himself.

Wringing his hands, Bon limped forward. "That's the end of today's competition. Please adjourn to your rooms. Dinner will be at six in the dining hall."

As everyone got up to leave, Instructor Verin gave V a small nudge. "Here's your chance to talk to Prince Seff," he whispered, before putting on his bucket.

She nodded and hurried after the prince, trailing him to the outhouse Kesh had just stepped into.

"I need to talk to you," she said.

"Sure, V," Prince Seff replied. "What about? Do you need help getting some more cupcakes? Or frosting?"

"What? No—I need to tell you something important."

"Okay, I'm listening."

"Not here, in *private*."

Prince Seff cast a quick glance at Kesh's outhouse. "All right, but we only have a minute or so." Lightly setting a hand on V's back, he led her a little ways off before coming to a stop. Visibly concerned, he folded both arms over his massive chest. "What's going on?"

Realizing there was no easy way of telling someone that someone else was trying to kill them, V just said it, "I believe Ha was poisoned and that the poison was really meant for you."

Surprise flashed across the prince's face. "You think someone is trying to kill me?"

"Yes."

Looking away, he rubbed a hand over his cheek and mouth.

"I'm sorry," she continued. "I'm sure that's the last thing you wanted to hear, but you need to know."

"And what leads you to believe this?" He looked at V again.

"The poison had to be in one of the cakes, and Ha ate the cake *you* were given."

"I see… I will have to consult with Kesh about this."

"No!" she exclaimed. "I mean… I don't know if that's a

such a good idea. Someone is trying to kill you and I'm not sure it isn't Kesh—what if he's upset with you about the war?"

He frowned. "You think Kesh tried to poison me?"

"It's possible, isn't it?"

Stepping closer to V, Prince Seff set his hands on her shoulders. "I appreciate you caring about me and trying to help, but I can handle this, all right?"

Shrinking under his piercing gaze, she said a reluctant, "All right."

"Thank you." Hands dropping to his side, he turned and walked away.

Watching him go, V caught sight of Kesh. Standing in front of the outhouse he'd just used, his dark eyes were fixed on her, clear anger flickering through them.

22

V stumbled into her room. The telly was on, and a newscaster was saying that the recent destruction of Praun, and the loss of Autia Noria, had encouraged Praun sympathizers to assist the prince in his war for civility. "I think… Kesh might… try to kill… me," she panted.

No longer wearing his bucket, Instructor Verin was sitting on a cot. "Kill you?" He flipped off the telly and looked at her. "Vivi, why would he want to do that?"

She kicked off her shoes and collapsed to the floor. Her legs felt like jelly from having sprinted up all forty-seven floors. "Because… maybe he… knows… that I… suspect that… he might be… trying… to kill… Prince Seff."

"We don't even know that he is—how did your conversation go?"

"Not… good." She shook her head and sucked in several lungfuls of air, finally catching her breath. "Prince Seff was hurt that I even suggested Kesh."

"Did you find out if he and Kesh were at the school?"

"Conversation never got that far."

"But you did ask him?"

"No."

Instructor Verin thoughtfully rubbed his nose. "What makes you think Kesh wants to kill you?"

"I saw him staring at me after he came out of the outhouse.

He looked *really* angry."

"And no doubt very sweaty and untidy."

"What?"

"From running up and down all those stairs."

"Huh?"

"Never mind. Don't you think it's possible he was angry because of the smell?"

"What?" V used the back of her hand to wipe the sweat from her forehead.

"The smell from the outhouses," explained Instructor Verin. "You don't think it was the smell that was making him angry?"

"Oh... No, I don't think so. He was looking right at me."

"So, he didn't look at Prince Seff at all?"

"I don't know. I just got up here as fast as I could."

"I see... did Prince Seff happen to touch you while you were talking?"

"He put his hands on my shoulders, but I don't see what that has to do with anything."

"Maybe nothing. Have you ever offered to shake Kesh's hand?"

"No. Why?"

"Well, Rohem culture revolves around certain traditions, one of which is that when a woman seeks a husband, she offers to shake the hand of the man she wishes to marry. If the man shakes her hand in return, the offer is accepted, and she becomes his wife."

V's brow furrowed. "So, you think that if I had, at some point, shaken his hand, I would now be his wife, which would explain why he looked so angry?"

"Yes. Rohems are very territorial, especially amongst

their own kind."

"Well, seeing as I *haven't* shaken his hand, and am therefore *not* his wife, that leaves us with no other explanation."

"Or maybe he's just having a bad day." Instructor Verin shrugged and handed something to V. "On a lighter note, this is for you."

"What is it?"

"A plant made out of green playdough?" he guessed. "It came with this." He held out a piece of folded green paper.

She took the paper and opened it. It said, 'Shhhh!' "What in the worlds...?"

"Before you got here, someone knocked on the door. When I opened it, Kesh was running away and those were on the ground. Now, if you'll excuse me, I'd like to go stare at myself in the bathroom mirror for a while." Instructor Verin stood up and walked into the bathroom, closing the door behind him.

V returned her attention to the green playdough plant; could it really be from Kesh? Had he somehow sneaked out of the outhouse, running all the way up to her room and back while she and Prince Seff were talking? But why would he have gone so far out of his way? Could it have anything to do with what he'd said about having a wife, but it was supposed to be a secret? Was this some sort of code for her to keep quiet? She didn't know. What she *did* know was that she needed some sleep.

Tucking the playdough plant and note into her dress pocket, she pulled herself onto the nearest cot where she found the yellow book. At the very sight of it, her stomach flip-flopped; earlier that day, Instructor Verin had told her he was close to deciphering the Unending Story's unique combination of imagination and creativity...

Suddenly, she was on her feet, running to the closest window. Without the slightest hesitation, she opened it, threw the yellow book out and watched it fall into the courtyard. Heart pounding, she was about to close the window when she noticed one of the articles had slipped out and was lying on the carpet. But that wasn't all, something was stuck to the back of it: Instructor Verin's worldmaker certificate! It had been in the yellow book the entire time—his meltdown, and her worry about being responsible for his death, had all been for *nothing*! Clutching the certificate to her chest, she crumpled up the article and threw it out the window, too. Satisfaction swelled within her, until she realized that both the article and the book would land in the very place she and Instructor Verin had to walk through to get to the teepee.

Uh-oh.

After a quick glance around the room, she ran to the telly, setting the certificate on top of it. She then ran to the door, and was just turning the handle, when Instructor Verin came out of the bathroom. At that very same moment, her stomach growled loudly.

"Yes, I too am famished," he said. "What do you say we skip dinner and take a little trip to that place...? What did Rainbow Jon call it? Guido's?"

V's stomach growled again; just the thought of real food was making her salivate. But what was she going to do about the book? She couldn't let him see it. "O...okay," she said, trying to think of a way to leave the Blue Sparkle that didn't involve going through the courtyard.

"Let's go then, shall we?" He headed for the door, his eyes

flickering to the cot. "Where'd my book go?"

"Uh..." V glanced at the window. "I found your worldmaker certificate."

"*You did?*"

"Yeah." She pointed to the telly.

"Thank goodness!" Instructor Verin sprinted over to it. "Now, no one will ever know!" he said, grabbing the certificate and stuffing it into his mouth.

Knock. Knock. Knock.

His attention diverted and he hurriedly swallowed. "Who could that be? Rainbow Jon to shine my shoes?"

Staring at him in disbelief—had he really just eaten his worldmaker certificate?—V stepped aside as he hurried to the door and opened it. Prince Seff was standing in the hallway. Kesh was right beside him.

"I suppose you're wondering why we're here," Prince Seff said, briefly looking at V.

"Nonsense," said Instructor Verin. "Clearly, you knew we were just heading out in search of food and have come here to join us."

The serious expressions on the Rohems' faces melted into wide smiles.

"Of course, we'll join you!" said Prince Seff.

"Great!" Instructor Verin clapped his hands together. "Let's go!"

23

Due to Prince Seff's brilliant idea of exiting the Blue Sparkle through the back doors—to avoid the masses of lurking reporters waiting to ask him about the Praun sympathizers—V was saved the task of creating a diversion to keep Instructor Verin out of the courtyard. Giddy with anticipation at the thought of having a real meal, she and the others made the short trek down the back alley and were soon seated at a booth inside of Guido's Soup, Salad, and Flatbread Bistro. Beside V, was Instructor Verin. Across from V, was Kesh. She shifted uncomfortably as the large Rohem stared at her; no longer did she worry he would kill her, but he still made her uneasy.

A waiter walked up to the booth. "Is this someone's bucket?" he asked, pointing to the floor.

"It's mine," said Instructor Verin. "I brought it with me in case of an emergency."

The waiter raised an eyebrow. "Emergency?"

"Yes. In case some Klouds with a capital K decide to drop in."

"Right." He pulled a pad of paper out of his apron. "What will it be?"

"Mmm…" Instructor Verin buried his face in the menu.

"I'll have one of everything," announced Prince Seff.

"Me too," Kesh said.

"Yes, me three," chimed in the instructor.

The waiter didn't appear at all fazed by the orders and trained his eyes on V. "What about you?"

V didn't know—there were simply too many options to choose from. "I guess I'll have the same as them."

Instructor Verin, Prince Seff, and Kesh gaped at her.

"What! I'm hungry, *too*." she declared.

"What about your cupcakitosis?" asked Prince Seff.

"I'll worry about that later," she replied.

"If that's all...," not even finishing the sentence, the waiter turned to leave and tripped over the bucket. The next few seconds ticked by in slow motion as he crashed to the floor and the bucket flew through the air, straight into the kitchen.

"Oh no!" someone shrieked. "A bucket just landed in the boiler!" An explosion followed and suddenly, the entire restaurant was on fire.

Instructor Verin, screaming and waving his arms in the air, scrambled onto the top edge of the booth.

"*What* are you doing?" V shouted.

"I'm getting out of here! Come on! It's not too late!" He grabbed her arm and tried to pull her up with him.

"Stop it!" She batted his hand away. "You're *not* helping!"

"Maybe this will help!" Prince Seff shouted over the hullabaloo. Reaching across the table, he seized the instructor and ran to the back door, tossing him outside. But less than a minute later, the instructor was back inside the restaurant.

"Go *outside*!" Prince Seff yelled as he slung two older women over his shoulder.

"No!" Instructor Verin yelled back. "I have to help save these innocent people!"

Meanwhile, V found herself being thrown over one of Kesh's shoulders. "What are you *doing*?" she exclaimed, the scent of cinnamon and something else—macaroons, maybe?—filling her nostrils.

"Getting you to safety!"

Everything was happening so fast that she didn't object. "Wait!" she said, seeing the storeroom. "Food!"

"Where?" demanded Kesh.

"There!" She pointed to a room stocked with real food and the Rohem veered inside.

Some while later, after Prince Seff and Instructor Verin had finished saving all the innocent people, and Guido's had burst into even more flames, and everyone was covered in soot and black smudges, they were back inside the Blue Sparkle. Sitting on the floor of V's and Instructor Verin's room, they were surrounded by open bags of fresh-baked flatbread, cheese, meat, sliced tomatoes, peppers, and lettuce.

The telly was playing in the background. On it, was Guido's Soup, Salad, and Flatbread Bistro—or what was left of it. Firefighters surrounded the building, spraying water from five different hoses. A newscaster was saying how no one was killed or seriously hurt, thanks to two men—one who strangely resembled a competitor from that baking show, the one with the name he could never remember, and another who resembled an assistant to one of the competitors. But, due to all the flames and chaos, no one could tell for sure who they were.

V glanced at the telly. On it, she clearly saw Prince Seff coming out of Guido's front door with six people in his arms. Instructor Verin was there too, running around in circles, screaming. Taking a bite of her sandwich, she redirected her attention to the Rohems. "You never told us why you came over, you know, before we went to Guido's?"

"You're right," Prince Seff said, swallowing a mouthful of meat. "Our earlier conversation by the outhouses got me thinking, and after counseling with Kesh, I, or should I say, *we*, have decided to let you in on a secret."

"A secret?" said Instructor Verin.

"What secret?" V finished her sandwich and reached for some more flatbread. As she did so, Kesh leaned over and touched her hand with one of his gloved fingers.

"I hope you liked the playdough plant," he whispered. "I made it just for you."

Unsure what to do, V just sat there. But then, Instructor Verin began looking for the salami, crawling over hers and Kesh's hands, breaking them apart. Hurriedly, she pulled her hand into her lap and trained all of her attention on Prince Seff.

"Earlier today…," the prince shoved an entire sandwich into his mouth, "…foo fay foo faf fom fill fee."

"What…?"

"Oaff…" Prince Seff swallowed. "Sorry, I'm just so hungry." He cleared his throat and patted a hand on his chest. "Earlier today you said that someone is trying to kill me, and you're right, but it's not Kesh. This I know for certain, he and I having been friends and cousins for nearly our entire lives."

V glanced at Kesh, who smiled at her through a mouthful of meat and cheese. Trying not to look disgusted, she forced a smile back.

"As I'm sure you've noticed by now," the prince went on, "Rohema is not exactly the model of peace. For millennia, our people have relished in physically bullying one another—you know, the typical pushing one another around, trying to show off who has the biggest muscles and such—but it never got too far out of hand. At least, not until three years ago when a new fad started, one that involved the tweaking of noses and tugging of ears. In and of itself, that doesn't seem like much, but when people started *losing* noses and ears..." he tapped the bubbly scar on the side of his head before pointing at Kesh's noseless face, "...I knew it was a problem. Others started to see it, too, and that's where the push for new laws of civility came into play. Unfortunately, due to some of Rohema's pre-existing laws, there was little I could do until a few months ago when I turned twenty-four. My time before then wasn't wasted, though. As I'm quite handy with computers and other forms of technology, I began work on a new line of bots to patrol our streets, and that's when I discovered a peculiar signal transmitting through our sector of the galaxy. Normally, I wouldn't have paid it much mind, but it appeared at the exact same time as the Planet Destroyer. I've been tracking it ever since."

"You *found* the Planet Destroyer?" V exclaimed, choking on a bite of sandwich.

Instructor Verin patted her on the back.

"I'm not certain," said Prince Seff. "But I've tracked the signal to this building and if my hunch is right, we should find a connection between it and the ship.

V was confused. "You think the Blue Sparkle and Planet Destroyer are connected?"

"Not the building per se, but the show, perhaps; it would take a great deal of money to build and maintain a weapon as technologically advanced as a ship that blows up planets."

"Are you saying that you think Palfrey Dolop is involved?" questioned Instructor Verin.

Prince Seff nodded. "I do have my suspicions: if it is Palfrey, and he knows why I'm here, it would make sense that he's the one trying kill me."

"There's no denying that something strange is going on with him and his show," Instructor Verin agreed.

"No, there isn't," said Prince Seff.

"So, you're being here was never about the show, or promoting peace, it was always about finding the Planet Destroyer?" asked V.

"Yes," admitted Prince Seff. "I've never baked before, so I was nervous about coming, but even if I'd been the first one eliminated, the show gave me a valid reason for being here. Luckily, baking hasn't been an issue."

Instructor Verin rubbed his soot-smudged nose. "Why didn't you tell anyone about the signal?"

"I wanted to, but I didn't want to make Rohema a target, so I decided to wait until I knew for sure what was going on and who was involved. But now that I've told you, you will help us, won't you?"

"That depends on what you plan to do next," said Instructor Verin.

"I was hoping to find out for certain whether or not Mr. Dolop is involved."

Instructor Verin rubbed his nose again. "How?"

"Well… he does seem to have a soft spot for V."

V's face turned red "Soft spot?"

Prince Seff nodded. "Yes. The smiles, the lingering handshake… Don't tell me you haven't noticed?"

V heard Kesh grumble something under his breath and her face turned even redder. "He probably just feels sorry for me, cupcakitosis and all. It's probably just for the show."

"Rubbish," said Instructor Verin, "Palfrey Dolop doesn't do things for people because he feels sorry for them."

"How would *you* know?" she retorted. "It's not like you know him. Besides, you had a bucket on your head."

"Perhaps I did have a bucket on my head, but I'm not deaf. Sure, as sure, you're our ticket in."

"But I'm already in, remember? You told me I have to break into his penthouse."

"Yes," said Instructor Verin, "but now that you've caught his eye, it might be better if, instead of *breaking* into his penthouse, you paid a *visit* to his penthouse instead."

24

V tugged on a damp curl; her body felt better after washing off the grime from the fire, but her mind was still an anxious mess. "I don't think this is a good idea," she said to Instructor Verin as they walked down the hallway.

"Of course, it is," he said. "No breaking and entering, no stealing anything—it's perfect."

"But I have no idea what to say."

"You say things to me all the time and do just fine."

"That's different—I'm not trying to discover whether or not you're a deranged psychopath."

"Because I'm *not* a deranged psychopath," he said, as they stopped beside the stairwell door. "You ready?"

"No." V glared at the floor; this was definitely the worst idea the instructor had ever had. Yes, she was there to help him spy so he would free her from the school, but this sort of spying was too advanced for her. She wasn't well spoken or smooth mannered, she was awkward. And yet, there she was, about to have a conversation with one of the most famous men in the galaxy while discreetly trying to unearth whatever secrets he was hiding—it made breaking and entering seem like fun. "Palfrey will figure out I'm a fraud and then drown me in the vat of frosting."

"No he won't—he likes you, remember?" Instructor Verin opened the door. "Don't forget in exactly one hour, Prince Seff will come by as a distraction in case you need a moment to snoop around."

"Okay," V grumbled, as she stepped into the stairwell. Pulling in a deep breath, she waited for the door to close and as soon as the latch clicked, made a mad dash down the stairs; she didn't have long and really needed to get that yellow book out of the courtyard. Upon reaching the main level of the Blue Sparkle, she ran through the lobby and out the front doors over to where it would have landed, but nothing was there. She started to worry that someone had taken it, but as long as that someone wasn't Instructor Verin, what did it matter?

Hurrying back inside, she ran up the stairs to the fiftieth floor. Heart banging inside her chest, she walked around for a few minutes to catch her breath, used the hem of her cupcake dress to wipe the sweat from her face, and then knocked on Palfrey's door. A few seconds later it opened. Palfrey was even more disheveled than before, his golden hair sticking out at odd angles, his button-up shirt buttoned incorrectly and completely untucked from his trousers.

"V!" Flashing a smile, he stretched an arm across the door frame. "What brings you here?"

"Uh…" She twirled a strand of hair around her finger and realized that she'd forgotten her spatula—what if she needed it to defend herself? "I guess I just wanted to say 'hi,' so, 'hi!'" She tried to run back to the stairwell, but Palfrey stopped her.

"Don't go," he said. "Come in for a bit. It's been a rough day: Ha's death, Guido's burning down… I could use some good company. Why don't you have some cashews with me?"

At the mention of Guido's, V was struck with a pang of guilt.

"They're real cashews," he went on to explain.

After some quick deliberation she consented; spatula or no spatula, she had a job to do. "Can I have some water, too?"

"Certainly." He guided her into the penthouse. "Water there's plenty of, it's food that's the problem; as I'm sure you've noticed, there's been a lot going on around here and it's caused a bit of a food shortage for the show. Even so, I've made it a priority to make sure you always have your cupcakes. Strange though, I'd never heard of cupcakitosis until you showed up, and to be honest, I was expecting a bit of a looney."

"A looney?" V was distracted by her surroundings; so far, she was standing in a very large, very empty room that smelled vaguely of onions. "Were you expecting only me to be a looney, or everyone to be a looney?"

"Everyone. Due to some recent projects, as well as the lack of food due to budget cuts, I thought it best to choose people who wouldn't notice or care that they weren't really baking. However, if you *do* care that you're not really baking, I whole-heartedly apologize."

V didn't know how to respond; did she say 'yes, I do care' and make it sound like she was normal? Or did she say 'no, I don't care' to meet the criteria of being a looney?

"It's okay," Palfrey said, guiding her into an adjoining room. "You don't have to say anything."

She smiled weakly and looked around; two of the room's walls were completely made of windows, the other two walls were bare, and aside from four folding chairs in the center of the floor, the room was empty.

"Have you ever been to Rohema?" Palfrey asked, holding out a folding chair for her to sit on.

"What?" V was taken aback; was he volunteering

information? Could her mission be so easy?

"Rohema," he said again. "Have you ever been there?"

"No," she said, sitting down.

He sat down across from her, his back to a windowed wall. "Well, there's no such thing as baking there. There are no ovens, stoves, microwaves, or kitchens. They eat food straight from the ground and don't bother to cook their meat. It's very primitive."

"Really?" She thought about Prince Seff eating an entire onion raw.

"Yes. Do you know much about them?"

"No. Just what you've told me and what I've heard on the news."

Frowning, Palfrey leaned over and patted a hand around his chair as though searching for something. "Excuse me a moment, will you?"

"Sure." Letting out a long breath, V slumped back in her chair; on the other side of the window-walls, Fooda's sun was setting over Delectabelia.

A moment later, Palfrey returned, handing her a cup of water and setting a plate of cashews on one of the folding chairs. "Please, help yourself."

"Thanks." She took a few gulps. "You must be very proud of yourself," she said, nodding to the outstretched city.

Palfrey barely glanced at the windows before scooping up a handful of cashews and popping them into his mouth. "I suppose it's okay," he said between chews. "I made this for the people, not for the joy of making something; our galaxy is so fast-paced now that if one can't find a way to both capture and keep attention, they won't go anywhere."

"Are you saying you didn't want to make Fooda?" She

took another gulp of water.

"Yes." He swallowed. "I suppose I am. I prefer natural beauty, but most people don't. And those that do, don't really appreciate it, if you get my meaning."

"Not really."

"Too many distractions: everything's high-tech and digital now. People experience the world through what they see on a telly, or a phone, but that's not reality. Reality is feeling the light and heat of a sun on your face and feeling wind and rain on your skin. Reality is having a face-to-face conversation with someone. Reality is a massive intertwining web of our environment and the people in it. I bet you almost anything…" He placed both forearms on his knees and leaned forward, "…that a simple native on the poorest planet in the galaxy has a richer, larger reality than any of the people who come to Fooda. The native may not travel to other worlds, or even travel beyond their own village, but no doubt he or she has a personal relationship with everyone around them, and with the land."

V put a cashew in her mouth and slowly chewed it; it was unquestionably odd that Palfrey, all on his own, had brought up the topic of Rohema; could he really be the one trying to do away with Prince Seff? And yet, the way he'd just spoken about reality and simple natives didn't seem characteristic of someone hell-bent on destroying planets.

"You know," he continued, "everyone thinks that being a worldmaker is a glamorous job—in my case, at least—but they don't understand how much work goes into it, how hard it actually is. Fooda was easy, considering it's just streets and restaurants with hotels. But real worlds, worlds with plants and animals and ecosystems are much, much harder and every detail must be accounted for. But no one cares about those worlds—not unless they can add some element of technology to it…"

Something on the other side of one of the window-walls caught V's attention. No, not something, *someone*: Instructor Verin. Her eyes widened; there were no ropes or harnesses tied around him—he was *free-floating*.

"…it's tough," Palfrey went on. "I just don't feel like I'm reaching my potential…"

Instructor Verin smiled at her before holding up two thumbs, a questioning look on his face. She quickly glanced at Palfrey; he was reaching for another handful of cashews. Locking eyes with the instructor, she nodded and then waved him away.

Palfrey sat up straight and looked over his shoulder. "Is everything okay?" he asked, turning back to V.

She nodded, her heart pounding; Instructor Verin had cut that way too close. "Yeah. Why do you ask?"

"It just looked as though you were waving at someone."

"Oh. Um, no. I was just…" she scrambled to think of an explanation, "…fixing my hair."

"And what lovely hair it is," Palfrey said kindly.

V wasn't sure if he was being serious or not but said a quiet 'thank you.'

Seconds later, a knock sounded on the door.

"Excuse me a moment, will you?" said Palfrey, getting to his feet.

"Of course." V watched him leave the room; had an entire hour already gone by since she'd barreled down the stairs? She knew she needed to get up and snoop around, but she was so tired. That, and there wasn't anything to snoop through—not unless Palfrey had some important clues taped underneath the folding chairs. Wearily, she got down on her knees and felt the underside of the chairs. Nothing. She'd gotten off her chair for nothing.

Tap, tap, tap.

Tilting her head back, she saw a vent in the ceiling. On the other side of it was a face. "Kesh?" she whispered. "What are you doing up there? Palfrey might see you."

Kesh held a finger over his lips and then pointed to the cashews.

"You want some cashews? What about all the food you just ate?"

"Still hungry."

She almost didn't believe him until she remembered how huge he was. Shrugging, she said 'okay' and grabbed a handful of cashews. Climbing onto her chair, she passed them through the vent.

"More," Kesh whispered.

"More?" She raised an eyebrow, but grabbed some more cashews and passed them to him. By the time Palfrey came back, she was sitting down again.

"My, you were hungry, weren't you?" he said, eyeing the mostly empty plate.

"Yeah. Sorry."

"Don't apologize. I'd be ravenous too, if all I had to eat were cakes, cupcakes, and pancakes. Good thing I like you, huh?"

V's cheeks grew warm, but this was no time to feel embarrassed; the prince's visit was a stark reminder that she needed more information and since there'd been nothing hidden on the underside of the folding chairs, she would just have to ask Palfry what she needed to know. "Forgive me for being so forward, but how do you feel about the Planet Destroyer?"

A few moments of silence passed before he responded. "Would you like to see the other worlds I've created?"

"I'm sorry?" She wasn't sure she'd heard him correctly; hadn't she just asked him about the *Planet Destroyer?*

"The other worlds I've created—would you like to see them?"

Before she could respond, Palfrey left the room. He returned shortly with a big leather scrapbook covered in ribbons and glittery stickers. The first few pages of it were photos of planets filled with vibrant colors swirling through breath-taking landscapes. After that, the photos changed, the planets becoming more industrialized and developed—more architecture, less nature; it was only the last handful she had even heard of. She then remembered Palfrey's interview on the telly a few weeks before, and the unhappiness that had been in his voice. "I'm sorry people haven't appreciated what you've done for them," she said. "If it's any consolation, I like your first planets the best—they're beautiful."

"Thank you." Chin trembling and eyes glistening, Palfrey excused himself from the room.

Feeling a twinge of sadness for him, V looked down at the scrapbook and flipped through it again. After Fooda, the pages were blank. There was, however, a galactic chart in the very back and scribbled at the top of it were two words, *destroyed planets*. Below that, several planets were circled in red.

"Dousen... Erra... Koun... Orouka... Hulse... Pelbok... Praun... Dort... Ton... Beboria... Rolk..."

Reading the planet's names aloud, it hit her just how

devastating and evil the Planet Destroyer was. Sick to her stomach, she closed the scrapbook and placed it on Palfrey's chair. After a few minutes of waiting for him to return, she got up and wandered around the room, spotting something on one of the walls she hadn't noticed before: a piece of white paper. Stepping closer, she saw it was Palfrey's worldmaker certificate. Tucked behind a plate of glass with no frame, it looked almost identical to Instructor Verin's. And yet... the more she looked at it, the more she realized it *was* identical. Right down to the insignia of Ton Worldmaker University and the year of graduation, minus the name written on it.

The interview of Palfrey that had previously popped into her head, popped into her head again, as did Instructor Verin's To Do list—the list on which he'd written the letters T.P.D.

25

Back in her room, V found Instructor Verin, Prince Seff, and Kesh shooting spitballs at the windows.

"So, how'd it go?" Instructor Verin asked. He shot one last spitball before walking over to her.

V's eyes narrowed slightly; she had a very big bone to pick with him, but it would have to wait until after the Rohems left. "It went okay. Palfrey's definitely acting strange, but I'm not convinced he's involved with the Planet Destroyer."

"Really?" Prince Seff shot another spitball before joining Instructor Verin. "You didn't see or find *anything* you thought was suspicious?"

"No. There wasn't anything *to* see or find—the entire place was empty."

"Did you ask him about the Planet Destroyer?" Instructor Verin questioned.

"Yeah, but he didn't answer, he just asked if I wanted to see the other worlds he'd made."

"He changed the subject? That's pretty suspicious if you ask me," said Prince Seff.

"I know, but that doesn't mean he's guilty," V replied.

Instructor Verin took out his comb, running it through his hair. "Are you defending him?"

"Of course not. I just don't think we should be condemning him if we're not one-hundred percent sure he's responsible."

Prince Seff sighed. "V's right. I've gotten so caught up in this whole thing that I've forgotten the first rule of being a prince: Never condemn unless there's mayhem."

"What does that even mean?" asked V.

"I'm not really sure," he replied. "But I do know that I need to take a step back and go over the facts again—maybe I missed something. Did Palfrey happen to give you any food?"

"Yeah, some cashews. But what does that have to do with anything?"

"Real cashews?" Prince Seff and Instructor Verin asked at the same time.

V glanced at Kesh, who was still shooting spitballs at the windows and every so often looking over to see if she was watching; evidently, he hadn't mentioned his little snack to the others. "Yes, but I don't see how that's important."

"But they're cashews," said Instructor Verin.

"Yes," said Prince Seff.

V stared at the two men, both of whom wore eager expressions on their faces. "I didn't bring any with me. Besides, you just ate all that food from Guido's."

"True," said Prince Seff, with a frown. "Well, since there aren't any cashews here, Kesh and I should be going. We may also conduct another investigation. No offense, V, but with entire planets hanging in the balance, we can't be too careful."

"None taken," she said.

"Good night, then." Prince Seff nodded politely before leaving the room with Kesh.

As soon as the door closed behind them, V turned to Instructor Verin. "T.P.D. That means *Trip Palfrey Dolop*, doesn't it?"

Instructor Verin's eyes widened and then dropped to the floor. "Yes."

Folding both arms over her chest, V said, "He's the one who tripped you and broke your nose, isn't he? He's the one who called you 'Mush Boy'."

"Yes," Instructor Verin said again.

"Why…" she let out a puff of air; she was trying not to be angry, "…why didn't you tell me?"

"I should have," he admitted, walking over to a cot and sitting down. "But I thought my knowing Palfrey wouldn't have anything to do with this case."

"Well, you thought wrong, because it *does*. And your hiding it makes me question whether or not your determination to spy on him has more to do with your little vendetta than with what's actually going on."

"I know, and I'm sorry." Instructor Verin's shoulders drooped. "I guess the main reason I never brought it up was because I didn't want to think about it; Palfrey and I weren't just worldmaker students together, we were best friends—until we went to TWU where we were required to put actual worlds together. That's when I discovered I couldn't make anything other than mush—gigantic messes of mush. Palfrey tried to help me, but it didn't do any good and after a while he started picking on me, tripping me, calling me names… I'll be honest, I was really hoping we'd find something on him simply because I wanted him to hurt as much as he's hurt me."

V let out another puff of air. "You should have told me—out of everyone you know, don't you think that *I* would have understood?" The instructor's eyes met hers and for the first time, she saw the resemblance between him and Ooblick. Surprisingly, it wasn't anything to do with the face, it was all to do with the hopelessness in the eyes; Instructor Verin, she realized, felt completely hopeless. Yes, he was gorgeous now, but that wasn't what really mattered to him. He wanted to succeed at something, only he never seemed able to do so—a feeling she understood all too well. "Listen," she said, stepping over to him. "I have no idea whether or not Palfrey's been blowing up planets, but there's still a chance he could be involved with Threka. And since he's invited me to have breakfast with him tomorrow, I'll have another look around and see what I can find. But even if I don't find anything, we can still help Prince Seff, okay?"

"Okay," Instructor Verin said, sounding miserable.

V patted his arm and looked out the window; it was dark outside. "I don't know about you, but I'm tired. What do you say we get a good night's sleep and then get back to work tomorrow?"

Knock. Knock. Knock.

"Hold that thought," she said, walking to the door and answering it. "Rainbow Jon, hi."

"Hi," panted Rainbow Jon. "This... for you." He handed her a small package wrapped in brown paper. "From... Secretary... Ophelia..."

"Thank you." V peeled back the paper: it was her slab. "Did she say why she sent it?" She looked up, but Rainbow Jon was already gone. Closing the door, she turned to Instructor Verin and saw that he'd turned on the telly. A flash news report of the Deluxe Worldmaker School For Worldmakers was playing and a reporter named Mitch was trying to interview Grula, but the cook wasn't cooperating,

"I'm in here all by myself now," she grunted. "Go bother someone else so I can finish making this food."

"What about that short, red-faced man who works in here with you?" Mitch asked.

Grula scowled. "You'll find *him* in the headmaster's office."

The camera cut out and when it came back on, Mitch was in Secretary Ophelia's office.

"Watch out for the hippopotamus," someone said in the background. "It's over by the window."

Avoiding the window, Mitch walked over to the secretary, who'd finally gotten her chair and card table down from the ceiling. Several minutes passed with him asking her questions, but to no avail. Eventually, he gave up and knocked on the headmaster's door.

"Come in!" someone said.

As Mitch entered the office, V nearly fell over when she saw who was behind the headmaster's desk, standing on his step stool. "*Jiji?*"

"Ah, here you are," Mitch said. "Just as the lady in the blue hip waders… what's her name?" He looked past the camera and someone whispered Grula's name. "Ah yes." he refocused on Jiji. "You're here just as Grula said you would be, but where's Headmaster Baz?"

"Didn't you hear? I'm stepping in as headmaster until a new one can be found," Jiji said, biting into a purple cupcake.

"You're the new *headmaster?*" V exclaimed.

"*You?*" Mitch said, shock ringing through his voice. "Where did Headmaster Baz go?"

"Got another job," Jiji said, crumbs spewing from his mouth.

"Wow…," Mitch cleared his throat. "So, what do you think after watching the most recent episode of the Baking

Adventures..." Uncertainty crossed his face. "Uh... Fun-Things-Happen...? Competition? How do you feel about your very own crepetosis-riddled, poem-yelping V having made it through the first three bakes?"

Crepetosis-riddled? Poem-yelping? V pursed her lips.

"I think she's done beautifully," Jiji said, taking another bite of cupcake, "just as I always knew she would. And when she comes back to the school, I shall ask her to marry me."

V's jaw dropped and she marched over to the telly, turning it off.

"That seems to be a reoccurring theme with you," Instructor Verin said glumly.

She whipped around to look at him. "*What* are you talking about?"

"Jiji..." Instructor Verin nodded at the telly and then looked at the door. "Kesh..."

"Kesh?" Her already tight stomach tightened even more. "What do you mean, *Kesh*?"

"I only suspected earlier, but now I'm certain he thinks you're his wife."

"*What! How?*"

"I don't know, I'm just telling you my conclusions from having observed him."

Undergoing a sudden onset of nausea, V said, "I'm going to go vomit now, after which I will brush my teeth. If this telly is back on when I come out of the bathroom, I will throw it out the window." She almost added, *just like your book.*

26

The following morning, V awoke on her cot. She'd remembered to pull it to the opposite side of the room from Instructor Verin's cot and had thus gotten a fair amount of sleep. Albeit, it was filled with nightmares of waking up beside Jiji or Kesh (sometimes both) on the day after their weddings, and having hundreds of very short, or very large, hot-tempered children. She rubbed her forehead; it was beaded in sweat. She looked at Instructor Verin's cot, hoping that seeing his face would choke out the images in her mind, but the cot was empty. A dismal song was coming from inside the bathroom, though.

She shuffled over to the bathroom door and knocked. It opened and her eyes widened; Instructor Verin was fully clothed, but dark circles lined his eyes, his hair looked just like a rat's nest, and he was holding his toothbrush like a microphone.

"Oh, hi Vivi," he said, sounding quite depressed.

"Instructor Verin, are you okay?"

"Of course. Why would you even ask?" He set his toothbrush on the edge of the sink. "I'm done. The bathroom's all yours."

"Wait." V put a hand on his chest to stop him from stepping past her. "Because…" Her voice faltered as she almost said, *because you are my friend and because I care about you, I cannot let you be seen like this in public.* But, were they really friends? Did she really care about him? And did he really care about her? "I..." She swallowed the lump in her throat and tried again. "... I can't let you be seen like this." Walking him to his cot, she sat him down and began combing his hair. But the comb kept getting stuck, so she tied the mass of snarls into a short, ratty ponytail. "This will just have to do. You still look gloomy, but you also still look very handsome." She wanted to add that everything would be fine, to not let Palfrey get to him, and that they were sure to find something on Threka. But truth was, she didn't know if they *would* find anything on Threka, nor did she know how to help with his long past friendship. And she certainly didn't know if everything would be fine.

***

Up in the penthouse, a grand breakfast of crackers and peanut butter had been set out on one of three folding chairs in what had been termed the 'dining room.'

"Again," said Palfrey, who looked as though he'd slept in his clothes and hadn't bothered to comb his hair. "I do apologize for the food shortage. And I'm sorry I don't have any cupcakes for you—Bon has them and will give them to you at the start of the show."

"It's okay," V said, trying to sound downhearted. Didn't it bother him that cupcakes were wrapped in recycled toilet paper? She was tempted to ask, but didn't want to get Rainbow Jon in trouble.

Palfrey smiled, but it was a distracted, stressed-out sort of smile; he wasn't as focused on her as he'd been the day before, his fingers tapping on the tops of his thighs, his eyes darting to a telly on the wall. "I hope you don't mind," he said, glancing at his watch. "I always catch the morning news and it should be coming on any moment."

"Not at all." She was glad for the distraction.

Standing up, Palfrey turned on the telly. A commercial was playing for a pet-mess vacuum. "V?" he said, "While this is on, I'm going to send a pigeon with a message to a construction crew, telling them to get Guido's repaired today."

She had never heard of sending birds with messages before, but as there were no phones around, didn't question it. "Okay."

"I won't be long," said Palfrey as he left the room.

After waiting a few seconds to make sure he wasn't coming right back, V began her search for something suspicious. But, other than a telly, three chairs, and a paper plate with crackers and peanut butter on it, the dining room was empty. Wondering if she'd overlooked something, she paced around, listening as the commercial for the pet-mess vacuum droned on and on. Finally, it ended, and the news came on,

"Greetings, galactic inhabitants," a man with dark-blue hair said. "We have quite a bit to get through this morning, but we'll start with the reminder to keep your tellys tuned in to the Baking Adventures A-B-C-D-E-F-G Competition later today—it's definitely the most intriguing episode yet. We also have an update on the Guido's fire that happened yesterday on Fooda."

A picture appeared on the wall behind him. In it, a large group of people were huddled together on the roof of a very tall, sparkly, purple building.

"This group of people was discovered late last night on the roof of this very tall, sparkly, purple building. According to them, they were eating in Guido's when the fire started, trapping them inside until one of the outside walls opened like a door and they floated to the top of the building. All of them are unharmed and grateful to be alive."

Floated? A smile tugged at V's lips. Instructor Verin may have been screaming and running around in circles, but she knew he was the one responsible for saving all those lives.

"As for this next set of news, I am grieved to tell you that another planet was lost late last night: Oruka. The ancient water world was the eleventh planet to fall victim to the dreaded Planet Destroyer and nearly four billion lives were lost."

27

It wasn't long after her breakfast with Palfrey, that V was back inside the teepee "baking." But something was bothering her. So much so, that she didn't notice when Truj grabbed the green playdough plant out of her pocket and ate it. Thankfully, Kesh didn't notice either, but even if he had, she wouldn't have cared because, aside from the unknown bother, there were a lot of other things bothering her, too. Things like someone trying to kill Prince Seff and killing Ha instead; another planet being destroyed; all of her nightmares of marrying Jiji and Kesh; and the tray of twenty-four cupcakes sitting on her baking station. But the unknown bother, whatever it was, was *different*.

From the corner of her eye, she looked at Instructor Verin. Having found another bucket—his last one being destroyed in the Guido's fire—he'd plopped it on his head and hadn't said a word since leaving their room, which was nearly an hour ago as she was almost done with her first bake. A loaf of sweet bread was what it was supposed to be, and she had one hour and seven minutes to make it. But again, there was nothing to bake with so she'd been mindlessly kneading playdough, the unknown bother painfully jabbing away at her insides as she did so. Attempting to think about something else in hopes that the bother might finally make itself known, she tried to complete her imaginary mission of saving the Sapphire of

Kirsh. But it was no use—the bother was too great. If only she knew what it was…

A loud thump sounded, and she startled—Instructor Verin had fallen off his trash bin and was snoring loudly on the floor. Biting the inside of her cheek, she quickly made sure his bucket was firmly on his head, and that he was splayed out in a somewhat comfortable position, before returning to kneading playdough. Not long after, Palfrey entered the teepee. Mostly, he looked the same as he had earlier that morning: wearing clothes from the day before, greasy hair spiked out in some places and flattened to his head in others… His smiles were gone though, and his brow was furrowed in such a way as to make him look like he had one monster of a headache. His blue eyes glanced over the competitors, and when they landed on Prince Seff, something that might have been nausea rushed across his face.

"All right," he said abruptly. "Everyone, bring up your bakes."

No one moved.

V's forehead wrinkled in confusion.

"Everyone, bring up your bakes," he said again, voice rising.

"All of us at the same time?" Stuarp asked.

"Yes," Palfrey replied with audible impatience. "Everyone at the same time."

"But then I won't be the center of your attention!" Elba cried.

"Let me rephrase this," said Palfrey. "If you don't bring your bake up here, along with everyone else's, you will be *disqualified*."

Elba's face flushed bright red and she looked as though

she was about to scream.

"And if you scream or throw any sort of tantrum," he continued, "You will also be *disqualified*."

Lips snapping shut, Elba carried a tray filled with massive wads of blue gum up to the dishwasher box.

Picking up her kneaded lump of playdough that looked nothing like any sort of bread she'd ever seen before, V followed suit.

Over the course of the next few minutes, the other competitors made their way up to the dishwasher box. Prince Seff had a lump of playdough with a half-eaten onion stuck inside of it, Stuarp had a handwoven paper loaf, Truj had a piece of linty candy from his or her pocket, Kesh had his spare nose patch, and Laquat had her false teeth again,

"I found this in the trash yesterday," she said. "I think it will taste delicious."

Palfrey's nose wrinkled in disgust and he turned to Elba. "Tell me about your loaf."

"This is my sweet bubble gum bread," the little girl replied.

Palfrey didn't say anything before moving on to Truj's piece of linty candy next, and then going around the crowded box to ask about everyone else's bakes.

"Looks good," he said, looking as though nothing looked good at all, because nothing did. "You all passed." He turned to Rainbow Jon. "A word before I go."

"Okay." Rainbow Jon lowered the camcorder off his shoulder.

As the two of them walked away, the competitors stood motionless—more than likely from shock at being told, yet again, that no one was being sent home.

Finally, V went back to her trash bin.

A good half-an-hour later, which involved Laquat hobbling around in search of her diamond teeth, and Truj attempting to stick Elba's wads of gum to the sides of the teepee, and Elba screaming at him or her to stop, everyone else made it back to their trash bins, too.

Bon limped forward then. "The next bake begins in seven minutes." With a trembling hand, he reached up and straightened the bandage on his head. "You will have exactly four hours to bake four identical, delicious looking cookies."

Incredulous, V looked at Instructor Verin. He was still asleep. Next, she looked at Prince Seff and raised an eyebrow. Four hours to make four cookies? If he understood her thoughts she couldn't tell, but he did shrug. Looking down at her baking station, she wondered what she was going to do for four whole hours. Tapping her fingertips on the countertop, she waited for the seven minutes to be up.

After what seemed more like fifteen minutes, Bon, who'd been aimlessly limping back and forth, threw his hands in the air. "Where is Rainbow Jon?" he demanded to know. "He was supposed to be here eight minutes ago! How are we supposed to keep the show's schedule if he's late?" He looked around as though someone had an explanation of where Rainbow Jon was.

No one did.

"Then there's only one thing to be done: we must all look for him." When no one moved, he stamped a foot and yelled, "Everyone, look for Rainbow Jon! The bake cannot start without him! He's got the camcorder, so without him, you will *not* be on the show!"

Suddenly, everyone was scurrying around the teepee

looking for Rainbow Jon. Elba was crawling on the floor, looking through the ovens and proving drawers. Head tilted back, Truj was calling out Rainbow Jon's name as though he or she expected to see him up amongst the teepee poles. Laquat was rummaging through everyone's pockets. The Rohems were marching around, squabbling about who would eat the last onion in Prince Seff's pouch, with Kesh saying he was older and should therefore get it. Stuarp was looking beneath the turned-over trash bins. And V was sitting at her baking station, wondering if someone should be searching the Blue Sparkle.

Suddenly, a horrible, bone-chilling scream came from the storeroom.

V, who was closest to it, jumped to her feet and ran inside. There, she found Bon huddled beneath one of the shelves, ghostly pale and shaking all over. "What is it?" she asked, hurrying to him.

Bon pointed a shaky finger at a drop cloth on the other side of the room. Sticking out from under it was the camcorder.

"Oh, no," V breathed. Approaching the drop cloth, she slowly reached down and pulled it back.

Staring up at her, were the dead eyes of Rainbow Jon.

28

Seated on her turned-over trash bin, V stared unseeingly into the center of the teepee as Elba made several attempts to steal Kesh's gloves, Laquat chased Bon around in circles, and Truj cut holes into the sides of the dishwasher box. But then, Instructor Verin began mumbling something from inside his bucket,

"First, Ton, then Beboria, Rolk, Pelbok, Dousen, Erra, Koun, Hulse, Dort, Praun, and now Oruka. Only ancient worlds... But *why*?"

Ears pricking, V turned to him. He was sitting beside her, hunched over like a defeated, old man. "What did you say?"

"Mmm?"

"What you just said—can you say it again?"

"About the planets?"

"Yes."

"I said, first Ton, then Beboria, Rolk, Pelbok, Dousen, Erra, Koun, Hulse, Dort, Praun, and Oruka." He ticked each name off on his fingers until he got to Oruka because he'd run out of fingers.

"Oruka—that was the planet destroyed last night."

"That's right."

"And yet...," V's stomach dropped as a horrible realization hit her.

"What is it?" Instructor Verin seemed to perk up.

V tried to take a breath, but it was more of a strangled gasp. "In the scrapbook Palfrey showed me yesterday, there was a list of all the worlds destroyed by the Planet Destroyer and *Oruka* was on that list."

"Huh?"

Figuring he must not have perked up as much as she'd thought, she went on to explain, "How could Palfrey have possibly known it was going to be destroyed last night unless he had something to do with it?"

A few, long seconds ticked by before Instructor Verin responded. "You're right," he said, understanding seeping into his voice. "It also explains why there's no food or furniture here—Palfrey's been selling it to fund the Planet Destroyer which Threka probably built for him! There *have* been rumors of them manufacturing illegal weapons, and that ship is *definitely* an illegal weapon."

V nodded. "Palfrey must have found out that Prince Seff was tracking its signal and tried to kill him with the poisoned cake, but accidentally killed Ha instead. And Rainbow Jon must have realized what happened, so Palfrey had to kill him, *too...*" The memory of seeing him lying dead on the floor, strangled with his own necktie, flashed through her mind and she shuddered. Seeing Ha had been horrible, but it was even worse with Rainbow Jon because she actually liked him.

"We need to get that list of planets you found in Palfrey's scrapbook," Instructor Verin said quietly.

V's heart started pounding. "Okay. When do I go?"

"You're not going anywhere. This is something I will take care of." He pulled Ursa's key out of his pocket.

"*You?*" V was stunned. "But you always make *me* do this stuff."

"I know, but this time it's much too dangerous, and I can't in good conscience make you do it." Instructor Verin stood up to leave.

"Wait!" she hissed, grabbing his arm. "You're not going right now, are you?"

"Yes."

"But what if something happens to you?"

"I'll be fine. Besides, I'm taking Prince Seff and Kesh with me."

"Oh." V couldn't hide the disappointment in her voice; she was the one who was supposed to be assisting him, not the Rohems. "Then what am *I* supposed to do?"

Instructor Verin raised the edge of his bucket and looked around the teepee. "Distract the others."

"Distract the others?"

"Yes. And if we're not back by the end of the bake, don't come looking for us, just…" he lowered his voice to a whisper, "…just contact Secretary Ophelia, she'll know what to do. And don't repeat her name—I can't risk anyone hearing it. If anything goes wrong, she's our only hope."

29

Roughly twenty minutes after Instructor Verin left with the Rohems, V *finally* thought of a distraction. She looked around the teepee: Stuarp was weaving; Laquat was napping; Elba was blowing a bubble; and Truj was lying on the floor, eating playdough. Sobbing loudly, Bon was staggering around, Giblit on his head and the camcorder in his arms.

Spatula in one hand, and a cupcake in her other hand, V climbed onto her baking station. "Can I get your attention, please?"

But no one even glanced her way.

Having expected as much, she tried again, but this time yelled, "CAN I GET YOUR ATTENTION, PLEASE?"

Almost instantly, Stuarp stopped weaving, Laquat woke up, Elba's bubble popped, Truj sat up, and Bon stumbled to a stop.

With all eyes on her, V held the cupcake high above her head and declared, "This sacred stone of power is known as the *Sapphire of Kirch* and it is my sacred duty to keep it out of the hands of Lord Raff, Tsar of the Dark World! Who is with me?" She looked at each of the competitors. When her eyes landed on Laquat, the old woman lifted her cane in the air,

"I will!" she crowed.

"Did you mean, *I am*?" asked V.

"Yes." Laquat reached into her mouth, adjusting her false

teeth. "Darn teeth! Always making me say the wrong thing!"

"Right. Anyone else?"

Elba raised a hand.

"Yes, Elba?"

"Will there be fighting? Will I get to punch people?"

"Not people—demons. And you can definitely punch them."

"Then I'm in." Elba blew another bubble.

"Me too!" announced Truj. "I'm going to use my ray-gun to kill every demon I see! Then, I will write a book about how their souls come back as dirty laundry!" He or she curtsied before squirting his or her mustard bottle "ray-gun" into the air.

V looked at Stuarp next. Of the remaining competitors, he was the only one who seemed uncertain.

"I like to promote peace, not violence," he said. "Violence is really bad for cloud conservation."

V wasn't sure what that meant but wished Instructor Verin had been there to hear him; clearly, not every Kloud with a capital K was the violent type. "If we don't fight, Lord Raff will control the Universe and there will never be peace again," she said.

After some moments of visible deliberation, Stuarp conceded. "All right."

"Thank you," said V, before turning to Bon. "What about you?"

"I think I'll just watch," he said, both looking and sounding exhausted. "This weekend has taught me that I really need a career change." He held up the camcorder. "I've always wanted to film movies, so perhaps this will be my start."

"Oh... okay." The thought of being recorded was a little

daunting, but as long as Bon and the others were distracted, V couldn't complain. Holding the cupcake high above her head again, and diving right into her mind realm, she announced, "I am the Sock-Mender, Lagatha! And with you, my newfound band of brave heroes, we must get to the Dark World's surface and rendezvous with the spaceship that will take us, and the Sapphire, to Crystalin!"

Everyone cheered, except for Bon, who put the camcorder on his shoulder and pushed the record button...

'... Holding her crochet hook with her teeth, Lagatha gripped the Sapphire in one hand. Her other hand was busy gripping outcrops of rock as she climbed the sheer cliff wall that led to the Dark World's surface. Being deep beneath the planet's crust was awful the first time. It was even worse the second time—the demons having stolen the Sapphire from her, throwing it back down there. Yet, not everything had been horrible—that's where she'd met her new comrades. The fate of the Universe no longer rested on just her shoulders, it now rested on four others' shoulders as well: Elba the Most Daring Girl Ever; Laquat, the Jewel Bedazzled Elder; Truj, the Wielder of the Ray-gun; and Stuarp, the Cloud of Peace.

Looking up, Lagatha saw that the surface was near, but the demons were near too, screeching furiously at having lost the Sapphire, *again*. Climbing faster, she emerged from the ground. Right behind her, was Elba, the Most Daring Girl Ever. Truj, the Wielder of the Ray-gun was next. He or she was followed by Stuarp, the Cloud of Peace, who was carrying Laquat, the Jewel Bedazzled Elder on his back. Greatly fatigued, all of them collapsed to the ground until the screeches of the demons intensified.

Crochet hook dropping from her mouth, Lagatha panted,

"That way!" She pointed to a dark, smoldering mountain in the distance.

Scrambling to their feet, the brave heroes ran or hobbled as fast as they could. For some reason, Truj, the Wielder of the Ray-gun, was doing cartwheels, but as he or she was keeping up, Lagatha didn't worry about it.

Suddenly, a fissure opened in the ground and a wave of the sickly, white demons surged out of it.

Elba, the Most Daring Girl Ever, shot sticky bombs at them, taking out half a dozen at a time. Truj, the Wielder of the Ray-gun, shot dozens more. Laquat, the Jewel Bedazzled Elder, used her Cane of Horrendous Hurt to clonk them on the head, killing them instantly. Stuarp, the Cloud of Peace, taught them yoga…'

"Wait a moment…" V cut in, disrupting the battle. "We're trying to *kill* them, not calm them down."

"But yoga *is* killing them—metaphorically, with *peace*," said Stuarp. "Everyone else has cool weapons, so why can't I have one, too? One that's peaceful?"

V thought for a moment. "Oh, all right…"

'… Back on the Dark World, while Stuarp, the Cloud of Peace, was subduing the demons with yoga, Lagatha put away her crochet hook and pulled out her largest pair of scissors—the same pair of scissors she'd used to cut off the head of the lava serpent. It was an absolute miracle she hadn't died then, either. But, just as she'd been falling into the lava, a gust of wind rushed by, tearing her from the grasp of the serpent's tongue, blowing her to land.

"Watch out!" bellowed Truj, the Wielder of the Ray-gun.

Lagatha jumped out of the way as he or she barreled past, exterminating several demons. Elba, the Most Daring Girl

Ever, was close behind with her sticky bombs. Rushing after them, Lagatha became a spinning whirlwind of cutting and slicing; heads flying here, writhing white bodies flying there... Before long, she and the other heroes were standing amidst a pile of twitching corpses.

"Where to next?" enquired Stuarp, the Cloud of Peace. Out of everyone, he looked the least tired and was actually smiling.

"There," panted Lagatha, nodding to the smoldering mountain.

"Excellent!" Stuarp, the Cloud of Peace, took off, jogging over the mounds of bodies.

Lagatha and the other heroes followed close behind and soon, they were staring up, up, up at the mountain. Only, it wasn't a mountain. It was a *tower*.

"We must climb this tower," said Lagatha, "The spaceship will meet us at the top."

Bravely, the heroes began the perilous climb, but it wasn't long before more demons attacked. Lagatha cried out as one jumped on her back, its claws digging into her flesh. But then, it was gone—Laquat, the Jewel Bedazzled Elder, and her Cane of Horrendous Hurt, had saved her!

"Ank Ooh!" Lagatha gasped, scissors in her mouth. But no sooner had the words escaped her than more of the demons attacked...

"I have to go to the toilet," Elba said, disrupting the climb.

"Eelly? I ow?" said V, spatula in her mouth.

"Yeah." Elba's nose scrunched up. "I have to go *real bad*."

"Ohay." Clinging to the side of the Blue Sparkle, V looked behind her and faltered; they were at least thirty stories high. Hurriedly, she grabbed the spatula out of her mouth and yelled,

"Attention everyone! Find the nearest window and go inside! *Right now!*"

Minutes later, they were all inside the building. V's heart was still racing at the thought of what had just happened, but she seemed to be the only one disturbed by it—everyone else was *smiling*. Even Bon, who'd somehow kept up with them, and Giblit, who was scratching his claws on the wall.

When toilet breaks were done, they resumed climbing the Blue Sparkle, only this time, V made sure they did so from the inside…

'… Having found a window in the side of the tower, Lagatha and the four heroes clambered inside, a dark, black staircase spiraling upward before them. As they began to climb, the demons could be heard clattering up the stairs, but Lagatha and the heroes were too fast. Soon, they reached the top of the tower, and glistening before them through the blowing soot storm, was the spaceship.

"Everyone on!" cried Lagatha.

Hurriedly, everyone climbed aboard and sat down.

Looking out the window, Lagatha saw the demons running toward the ship. If enough of them swarmed it, it wouldn't be able to take off and the Sapphire would never leave the Dark World. This was their only chance. "Pilot, take us to Crystalin!" she ordered.

Nothing happened.

"Pilot!" she ordered again. "Take us to Crystalin!"

"I think the pilot's dead," said Elba, the Most Daring Girl Ever.

"What?" Lagatha peered around the pilot seat. Sure enough, he was dead. "What do we do?" She was starting to panic; she didn't know how to fly a spaceship. Looking out the window again, the blood drained from her face: it was Lord Raff! He was coming for the Sapphire! "We need a pilot right now!" she shouted at the top of her lungs.

"I can be a pilot," Stuarp, the Cloud of Peace, said. Calmly climbing into the pilot's seat, he started the engine and lifted off the tower just in time. "So where exactly is Crystalin?"

"In a galaxy near the center of the Universe," Lagatha gasped, hands clutching at her heart—they had cut that *way* too close. She leaned around the pilot seat and punched in the coordinates. "We should be there in no time."

In no time at all, they were docked on a tiny island surrounded by miles of clear, blue water. Lagatha looked out the window, tears welling up in her eyes. Not tears of sadness, but tears of joy. The journey was finally over. After all the loss, pain, and time, it was *finally over*—thanks to her newfound hero friends. She couldn't have done this without them.

"So, what do we do now?" asked Elba, the Most Daring Girl Ever.

"Now," said Lagatha, "I take the Sapphire and bury it in the heart of the sea where it was taken from. There, no man, woman, or living creature will ever disturb it again, and peace and joy will permanently fill the Universe." An air of reverence fell over her and the heroes as she climbed out of the ship and dove into the water. Far below, was a mound of dark-blue stone, and inside the stone, a hole. Swimming down to it, she took the Sapphire and placed it inside. Immediately, the Sapphire melded in with the stone, making it perfect, making it whole. Finally, she thought, her mind going fuzzy from being underwater for so long, *it is finished*. She knew then that she was dying. Her body was suffocating, drowning. And she being the last of the sock-menders, well, people would have a hard time getting their socks mended from thereon out. But it was more than a fair trade—she was just happy knowing the Universe was okay...

Suddenly, a pair of hands grabbed her, pulling her from the water. Sunlight shone warmly on her face. She could breathe again. Blinking through bleary eyes, she looked up into the faces of her four hero friends.

"Sock-Mender, Lagatha!" they cheered. "You just saved the Universe!"'

30

"What is the meaning of this?" someone shouted.

V coughed, water spurting from her mouth. To one side of her was a furious looking Palfrey. To the other side of her was the water fountain. Standing near her feet were Elba, Stuarp, Laquat, Truj, Bon, and Giblit. "What happened?" she asked. Her throat was dry and her head throbbed.

"You just saved the Universe," Laquat said, hobbling to her side and putting the spatula in her hands. "Don't forget your scissors."

"Oh…" Memories of taking the Sapphire to Crystalin filled V's mind. "*Ohhh…*"

"What do you mean, V just saved the Universe?" Palfrey snapped. "And what does that have to do with ruining my teepee, vandalizing my building, stealing my hover-bus, and making a disaster of this courtyard?"

"What…?" V was confused, but then Stuarp helped her sit up, his cloud costume shielding her from the sun as she looked around. The Blue Sparkle was plastered in globs of playdough, paint, glue, glitter, and gum. The courtyard was more of the same, although it was hard to see all of it with the hover-bus docked nearby. And last, but not least, the teepee resembled a set of bones with flaps of skin hanging from it.

"And can anyone tell me what happened to the water fountain?" Palfrey pointed to the bubbling, gurgling pool of water. "Well? Doesn't *anyone* have an explanation for *anything*?"

"We did get a little distracted," said Bon.

"But we have some excellent cookies to show you," Elba reported.

Seeming somewhat pacified, Palfrey said, "All right, come show me and we'll deal with this mess later." He led the competitors into the teepee and ordered them to their baking stations. "Where are the Rohems?"

V's stomach lurched; she'd been so preoccupied by her most recent epic disaster that she'd failed to notice the Rohems weren't there. And more importantly, that Instructor Verin wasn't there. Had something happened to him? Had *Palfrey* done something to him? A loud snap pulled her from her thoughts. It was Elba's big, blue bubble popping.

"Prince Seff and Kesh must have been left behind on the Dark World," Elba said, blowing another bubble.

"Yeah, I think they died," added Truj.

A bewildered look crossed Palfrey's face. "Then I guess we'll go ahead without them. Elba, you're first."

"Hooray!" The little girl took a bottle of glue from Kesh's baking station and hopped up to the dishwasher box, handing it to Palfrey.

"What's this?" he asked.

"It's a bottle of glue made out of four cookies."

Palfrey brought the glue to his mouth and pretended to take a nibble. "Interesting," he said, not looking pleased, but not looking disgusted either. "Thank you, Elba. Laquat!"

Tottering up to the dishwasher box, the old woman set down a dripping wet, mushy cupcake. "This is the Sapphire of Kirsh cookies. I pulled it out of the water fountain."

"Sapphire of Kirsh cookies?" Uncertainty crossing his face, Palfrey picked up the cupcake and sniffed it before tossing it over his shoulder. "Thank you, Laquat."

Stuarp was next, presenting four empty containers of playdough. "I'm sorry," he said. "I was going to fill them with woven chocolate cream, but I ran out of time." Looking very apologetic, he picked up his "cookies" and went back to his trash bin.

"Truj!"

Truj unfolded a large piece of pastel-rainbow fabric decorated with spurts of yellow, white, brown, and red paint, glitter, smashed cupcakes, and lumps of playdough. "It's the four cookies mural," he or she explained.

"V!"

Between worrying about the instructor and watching the other competitors present their bakes, V had all but forgotten about her own. Thinking quickly, she picked up her empty tray and presented it to Palfrey.

"What's this?" he asked, eyeing the empty tray.

She anxiously sucked in a breath of air and silently ordered herself to keep it together; if Palfrey *had* done something to her friends, it was better if he thought she didn't know. "This is my tray of four invisible coconut-buttercream-lemon sugar cookies."

"Is that so?" Palfrey pretended to pick up a cookie and take a bite. "A bit bland, but not bad," he said. "You may go back to your baking station."

She did so, anxiously awaiting the announcement of who would be cut from the show so she could go look for Instructor Verin.

Leaning over the dishwasher box, Palfrey's light-blue

eyes scanned the competitors. "Since all of you have done a fairly decent job this round, I've decided not to eliminate anyone. As for the final bake-off, you will be making a fruit pie and you have one hour, starting now." Without so much as a goodbye, he turned on his heel and left the teepee.

The moment he was out of sight, everyone got to chattering, but not about their pies—they were chattering about their recent adventure of saving the Sapphire and started planning a *new* adventure.

"Aren't you going to join us, V?" Stuarp asked.

"I'd love to," she said, "but I've lost my assistant and need to find him." Spatula in hand, she ran all the way up to her room. It was empty. She ran to Prince Seff's and Kesh's room next. No answer. Slumping against the door, she knew then that there was only one place left they could be: Palfrey's penthouse. An awful feeling of dread swept over her; what was she to do? *Contact Secretary Ophelia*. Those had been Instructor Verin's last words to her.

She rushed back to her room and grabbed her slab. Hoping the secretary would read the next day's paper first thing, she did some quick typing and pressed the 'send' button. She then rushed up to the penthouse. The door was a crack open. Her heart skipped a beat.

"Palfrey?" she said, knocking on the door. "Palfrey?" She knocked again, the door opening wide enough for her to slip through. Neck prickling, she held her spatula out in front of her and stepped inside. "Palfrey? The door was o… *Instructor Verin!*"

The instructor was on the floor, hands tied behind his back.

V rushed to his side, brushing a strand of hair from his

cheek; his eyes were closed, but he was still breathing. Kesh was a few feet away, bound and gagged. Blood trickled down the side of his head.

"Kesh!" She hurried to the Rohem and pulled the gag out of his mouth. "What happened? Where's Prince Seff?"

Kesh groaned and pointed to an adjoining room.

She turned her head and saw Prince Seff sprawled on the floor, covered in blood. "Oh, no," she said, putting a hand on the carpet to steady herself. "What happened?"

"Palfrey," Kesh whispered.

A wave of nausea and dizziness hit her; if Palfrey could subdue a full-grown Rohem man, there was no telling what else he was capable of.

After hastily untying Kesh, she brushed a shaky hand across her forehead. "Go check on Prince Seff. I'll stay here with Instructor Verin."

Kesh nodded and got to his feet, running to the other room.

V got to work trying to wake the instructor and had just succeeded in getting his eyelids to flutter when the penthouse door slammed shut.

"What's going on here?" Palfrey shouted. Sounds of a scuffle followed.

Moments later, something hard hit V in the back of the head and everything went black.

31

V groaned and tried to move but couldn't. She groaned again, this time opening her eyes to a bright splash of sparkles. Quickly closing them, she tried opening them again, only much more slowly, and seconds later was staring up into a chandelier.

Where was she?

Hazily, she looked around; no walls, pillars of concrete, frosting smears everywhere… She was in the dining hall. But why? And why was she lying on a hospital bed, strapped to it with strips of pastel-rainbow fabric?

"Instructor Verin," she mumbled. "Instructor Verin, I need help. I don't know what's going on and…" Her memory cleared then, crashing over her like a giant, roaring wave. "Instructor Verin!" she exclaimed, violently wriggling around. He was hurt! She needed to help him! And the Rohems! They were hurt, too! Possibly even… dead. *"Instructor Verin!"*

"V, it's okay," someone said.

She stopped struggling and looked at the door. Prince Seff was shuffling into the room, a white bandage wrapped around his head. "Prince Seff! You're okay! But what happened? Where's Instructor Verin?" The words spilled from her mouth in a hysterical rush.

"Whoa there, not so fast." Prince Seff smiled and then winced, tenderly touching the side of his bandaged head with a bandaged hand. "Yes, I'm okay, and Instructor Verin is okay, too. He's got the all-clear from the medbot and is getting his shoes shined in the kitchen. As for what happened...," he paused and took a deep breath, "...Palfrey found us in his penthouse and used his worldmaking powers to subdue us. It was a good thing you came when you did and untied Kesh because he was able to escape and contact the PPC. As we speak, Palfrey's being arrested for the destruction of eleven planets and the deaths of billions of people—Ha and Rainbow Jon included. V, if it weren't for you, he'd still be on the rampage."

"Really?" Her stomach twisted into a knot; it was all too much, all too horrible to be real.

"Yes. Would you like to see?"

Swallowing hard, she nodded.

"All right, then." Prince Seff shuffled over, undoing the straps around her arms, torso, and legs. "The medbots had to put these on so you wouldn't fall off the bed as they carried you down the stairs," he explained.

The courtyard was a mess of commotion: PPC spaceships, flashing lights, inquisitive vacationers swarming the streets, reporters, cameras.... In the midst of it all, V saw Palfrey. More disheveled than ever, his hands were cuffed behind his back and two PPC officials were loading him onto a ship. The door started to close when he spotted her.

"V!" he cried. "Tell them I didn't do it! You know I had nothing to do with it! I loved those planets! V! You have to tell them! I'm being framed! Help—!" The door closed and the ship lifted off.

A muddle of emotions, V watched it soar away; part of her wanted to believe him, to help him, but the other part of her wanted him to pay for what he'd done. And not just for destroying eleven planets and killing billions of people, but for hurting Instructor Verin.

"Do you want to go back inside?" Prince Seff asked softly. She nodded.

The prince set a gentle hand on her shoulder. "I'll take you to your assistant."

A few minutes later, she was standing in a grand kitchen. But all that was left of the grandness was a stove-top oven, a refrigerator, and a table piled with bags of flour and sugar. There were a few chairs too, and sitting on one of them, getting his shoes shined by a medbot, was Instructor Verin. As soon as he saw her, his face lit right up.

"Vivi!"

Unable to stop herself, she ran over and gave him a giant hug. "I'm so glad you're okay!" she said, wiping a stray tear from her cheek. Letting go of his neck, she moved back a few inches to look at his face. "I thought something terrible happened to you!"

Instructor Verin looked happy, but also a little confused. "Spotted apple buffalo?"

"What?"

"Oh," said Prince Seff. "I should have told you—Palfrey hit him in the head pretty hard and he's been a bit mixed up since."

"But you said he had the all-clear."

"He does, and he'll completely recover, it'll just take some time. It was a bit strange though... you were still unconscious when he woke up and we had to put you in the dining hall because he kept trying to paint your toenails. The only way we could distract him was by getting this medbot to shine his shoes."

Eyebrows raised, V looked at Instructor Verin. "I thought you hated feet, and that painting someone else's toenails was a horrible punishment."

He looked confused again, but then shrugged and smiled. "Hillbilly sock worm gobble!"

32

It was well past midnight, but V hadn't gotten a wink of sleep. Instructor Verin, on the other hand, was peacefully snoring away on his cot. It wasn't an ideal situation, remaining in the Blue Sparkle, but, due to all the attention from the news media, she and the other competitors had been advised to stay until the mobs of outraged Fooda vacationers died down. Surprisingly, only half the mobbers were angry that Palfrey was the culprit. The other half were angry because they believed he'd been accused unjustly.

But what did she believe?

She didn't know—not anymore. What she *did* know was that all the evidence pointed to Palfrey. And yet, the unknown bother from the day before was bothering her again. It had temporarily dissipated once Palfrey had been arrested and she'd gotten Instructor Verin back safe and sound. But the moment the two of them had stepped into their room it returned, and it made her wonder if she'd missed something. Looking at the instructor, she wished he were awake so she could talk to him, but he didn't show any sign of waking up. And it was just as well because, with his head injury, he needed all the sleep he could get.

Scooting to the end of her cot, she turned on the telly. Just as she'd suspected, most of the stations were flashing reports on Palfrey, showing him being arrested and taken away by the

PPC. On one of them, she even heard him shouting to her that he was innocent, that he'd been framed. She quickly changed the channel, flipping through until she found a station that didn't have his picture plastered all over it,

"And so," said a newsman with periwinkle hair, "over the past twelve hours since this story was found and posted on the web for the entire galaxy to read, it has become an instant phenomenon."

A picture of a man appeared and V immediately recognized him as the man who'd cheered her on for spitting her cupcake on the ground, and later thanked her for doing so: it was Cannon. His picture turned into a newsreel,

"Until a few days ago," he said, "I was endeavoring to make a company that sold cupcakes as fertilizer, but when I saw that yellow book fly out of one of the Blue Sparkle's windows, I knew it was providence. So, I jumped the fence, ran across the courtyard, and snatched it up."

"And you'd never heard of the 'Perpetually Unending Story' articles before?" a woman with a microphone asked.

"No."

"And you have no idea who wrote them?" she pressed.

"No," he said again. "I checked with the newspaper it's printed in and was told that it has an anonymous author."

"Well, whoever he or she is, they're certainly going to be one of the wealthiest persons in the galaxy. But you've made a bit of money off it, too, isn't that, right?"

"Yes, the number of hits on my website have been astronomical..."

The interview continued for a few more minutes, but it wasn't until a jingle for a pet-mess vacuum came on, that V realized her mouth was hanging open; her plan to get rid of the yellow book had backfired in the hugest way possible—how was she going to explain this to Instructor Verin?

Following a few more pet-mess-vacuum commercials, the newsman with periwinkle hair returned to the telly,

"Thank you for that intriguing story about the 'Perpetually Unending Story' articles. Now, back to the most humongous, mind-blowing story we've ever had: the infamous worldmaker, Palfrey Dolop, turning out to be a deranged, psychotic, planet murderer."

A picture of Palfrey appeared.

"Oh, how appearances can be deceiving—all this time we thought Mr. Dolop was pro-planet, but it turns out we were all wrong…"

Both saddened and sickened—not only by Palfrey, but also by the discovery of the yellow book's fate—V turned off the telly before getting up and wandering out into the hallway. Turning a corner, she almost tripped over Stuarp. This wasn't his usual floor, but under the circumstances, the competitors had decided it was best if they stuck together. As such, Elba, Laquat, Truj, Stuarp, and even Bon, had moved into a section of rooms down the hall from Prince Seff's and Kesh's room.

"Stuarp?"

Stuarp, who was sitting on the floor, stretching, looked up. "V!" A smile brightened his cloud-wreathed face. "I take it you couldn't sleep either?" He straightened his rose-tinted glasses.

Even beneath his bright smile, V could see the same feelings of shock, horror, and sadness she felt inside. "Pretty much."

"Would you like to do some stretches with me?"

"No thanks."

"What about food? We could make something in the

kitchen."

She hesitated; her stomach *was* rumbling, so, as long as the food didn't touch any parchment paper or cupcake wrappers, it was probably worth a try. "Yeah, let's do it."

A short time later, the two of them were in the kitchen when V heard voices in the hallway. Certain they belonged to a few troublesome reporters, she took hold of Stuarp's arm and pulled him into a nearby closet. Shutting the door most of the way, she left a small crack to see through.

"What's going on?" Stuarp asked.

"I heard voices. I think it might be some repor—"

Suddenly, the kitchen door swung open and Prince Seff walked in, followed by Kesh. They headed straight for the refrigerator.

Clearly wrong about the reporters, V was about to step out of the closet when a third person entered the kitchen: Headmaster Baz. Stifling a cry of surprise, she clamped a hand over her mouth—what was *he* doing there? Beside her, Stuarp was reaching for the door handle. "No," she whispered, dropping her hand from her mouth and grabbing his arm "Something isn't right."

Silently, Stuarp scrunched up beside her and together, they peeked through the partially open door.

"You've done very well," Headmaster Baz said, walking over to the Rohems. Prince Seff, who was no longer wearing any bandages, had taken an egg out of the refrigerator and was eating it raw. Kesh, who was no longer wearing his nose patch, or his gloves, had grabbed a stick of butter and was eating it like a candy bar.

V grimaced at the sight of Kesh's scarred, noseless face, but then couldn't help noticing his hands, and that one of them only had four fingers. Before she could stop it, a terrible word burst from her mouth; if what Instructor Verin had told her was true, then she really *was* Kesh's wife!

"V!" hissed Stuarp. "You shouldn't say things like that!"

"I know!" she hissed back. "It just popped out!"

"Now that the problem's been taken care of," Headmaster Baz was saying. "I suppose you want the *zaret*."

"You found it?" said Prince Seff.

"Of course, I did. Don't treat me like a decrepit idiot—I always find what I'm looking for."

"Well? Where is it?" Prince Seff asked, excitement in his voice.

"In a safe place. And I'll give it to you, once you pay me what's due."

"That wasn't the deal; you get what was promised when you give me the zaret."

"That was the *original* deal, but seeing as how you've hoodwinked everyone around you, I'm not sure you won't try to do the same to me."

A moment of silence passed. "All right. I'll give you what was promised, but only on the condition that we give each other what we want at the exact same time."

"Agreed," said Headmaster Baz.

Prince Seff pulled an onion out of his pouch and started eating it. Kesh finished the stick of butter and grabbed an egg, shoving the entire thing into his mouth.

"Ek," said a disgusted looking headmaster. "Between watching you..." he pointed at Prince Seff, "...eat those decrepit onions, and you..." he pointed at Kesh, "... shoving whatever raw food you can find into your mouth, I'm going to be sick!" He turned and headed for the kitchen door, but before he got there, Truj lumbered in and went to the refrigerator, grabbing a cupcake.

"Those are for V," said Prince Seff. "They're for her cupcakitosis."

"No, she has lemonbarititis," Truj said, cradling the cupcake to his or her chest.

Prince Seff raised an eyebrow.

Headmaster Baz snorted and tried to leave again, but then, Laquat hobbled in.

"What are you hoodlums doing in here?" She croaked. "Not trying to steal my lapis nose ring and tanzanite tooth, are you?"

Truj was the only one who responded. "No."

"You'd better not be." Laquat went to the refrigerator and got a cupcake.

Looking most inconvenienced, Headmaster Baz made another attempt to leave when the door opened a third time. It was Elba.

"Oh, hey," she said, blowing a bubble. "Are you having a party?" She too, went to the refrigerator.

Visibly annoyed at this point, Headmaster Baz opened the door just in time for Bon to shuffle in. Donning a pair of pastel-rainbow pajamas, Giblit was perched on the top of his bandaged head.

"Hello," he said glumly. "I suppose everyone got hungry at the same time?" He shuffled toward the refrigerator but was abruptly stopped by Prince Seff.

"Not so fast."

Bon looked confused. "Why not? Are there laws regarding how fast one can walk to a refrigerator?"

Before the prince could reply, Headmaster Baz spoke,

"Let him go, Seff."

"No. Out of everyone here, he's the only one smart enough to connect us."

"It will only cause trouble and I *hate* trouble."

"More trouble than if he goes blabbing to someone about what he saw?" Prince Seff turned to Kesh. "Take Bon to the vat of frosting and drown him."

Kesh shoved another egg into his mouth and took a step forward, but then, Bon started laughing. It was a high-pitched, nervous, sort of laugh.

"Why are you laughing?" Prince Seff asked with exasperation. "There's nothing funny about dying."

"I know," gasped Bon between laughs. "But we don't really use the vat of frosting to drown people. I merely put that into the contract to deter those who aren't serious about being on the show. Quite clever, isn't it? Palfrey doesn't even know it's there—I snuck it in!"

"Well, that's a disappointment." Prince Seff shooed Giblit off Bon's head and gave the middle-aged man a good thump with his fist, knocking him unconscious. Immediately after, Elba started screaming so he thumped her on the head, too. He then turned to Truj, who tried to run away, but slammed into a wall, knocking himself or herself out. "Where's the other one?" he asked, looking around the kitchen. "Laquat, where'd she go?"

"I'll find her," said Headmaster Baz. "But this decrepit idea of yours had better work."

"It will. I didn't come this far to fail."

"I sure hope not," the headmaster said, walking out the door.

Prince Seff scanned the room again.

"What are you doing?" asked Kesh.

"It's possible the old woman is still in here," the prince replied, walking around the table, refrigerator, and oven before moving toward the closet.

Instinctively, V shrank back. Beside her, she felt Stuarp doing the same. "We have to hide behind something," she whispered to him.

"The closet's empty," Stuarp whispered back. "There's nothing to hide behind."

A second later, the door opened, and V found herself staring up into the dark eyes of Prince Seff.

33

V couldn't help noticing how Prince Seff's face had changed; his warm eyes cooling to ice, the soft lines around his mouth hardening to stone... She shuddered as he paced past the pole that she, Stuarp, Bon, Elba, and Truj were tied to. They were in the basement of the Blue Sparkle, only, she didn't know how long they'd been there. What she *did* know was that her head ached something awful where the prince had thumped her with his fist, rendering her unconscious. The rest of her body ached too, probably from being dragged down the stairs.
Her eyes flickered to the other side of the basement where a worried looking Kesh was stirring a ginormous vat of frosting with a broken piece of pipe. Suddenly, the Rohem's eyes riveted on hers and she realized with a jolt that he *was* worried—about her. She was his wife, after all. It made sense now: his standing by the curtain to keep her hidden, his whisperings to her after she'd run into him and knocked herself out, the way he'd scowled when Palfrey had shaken her hand, the anger in his eyes when Prince Seff had touched her, the green playdough plant and note he'd made for her... He was the hooded man she'd offered to shake hands with and he'd accepted. She hadn't known that was a marriage ritual, but Headmaster Baz had, which was why he'd told Kesh that she didn't know of their customs. Quite obviously, Kesh hadn't listened, taking their handshake to heart.

"Hey," Stuarp whispered, nudging V with his elbow. "Isn't that your spatula?"

Tearing her eyes from Kesh, V followed Stuarp's gaze to Prince Seff's belt and her jaw dropped. "Yeah," she said, feeling miffed; her spatula was important. Albeit, she got annoyed carrying it around all the time, but it had come in handy as a crochet hook, and as a pair of scissors. "What's *he* doing with it?"

Stuarp shrugged. "I don't know."

"Is the frosting ready yet?" Prince Seff called out. Still pacing back and forth, he pulled an onion out of his pouch and glowered at it.

"Hey, Prince Seff," said Elba. "You don't like allium cepas, do you? Allium cepa is the real name for onion—I just learned that in my Youngsters for Radical Forms of Agriculture class."

The glower on the prince's face redirected to the little girl. "Of course, I don't like them; they're hot, pungent, and they make my breath smell awful. They're the *real* reason Autia rejected me—she couldn't stand the way my breath smelled and there was nothing I could do about it. It's not easy being a victim of *alliumcepatitis.*"

Alliumcepatitis. V had heard that term before—when she and Instructor Verin were in the pantry spying on Headmaster Baz and his two friends. Just as she'd suspected, Kesh was one of those friends. And Prince Seff, well, he was *definitely* the other friend. The pieces of the puzzle were finally falling into place: both men were Rohem, were constantly squabbling, knew Headmaster Baz, *and* Prince Seff had alliumcepatitis—*allium cepa* being another name for *onion*... Mind jumping into a reeling, wheeling, whirring of thoughts, she remembered back to when she'd been hiding in Headmaster Baz's office, and how she'd overheard him tell the man beside him—the man she now knew had been Prince Seff—to make sure *he* took the fall for something... "It was you all along, wasn't it, Prince Seff?" she blurted out. "You're the one controlling the Planet Destroyer! You and Kesh and Headmaster Baz are all in on it together! You didn't come on the show to find it, you came on the show to frame Palfrey—he's been tracking it, hasn't he? And he must have gotten close or else you wouldn't have bothered coming here..." Her voice faded as she realized something else. "You staged the whole thing in Palfrey's penthouse, didn't you? *And* you killed Ha and Rainbow Jon!"

Elba, Stuarp, Truj, and Bon gasped.

Clap. Clap. Clap.

"Very good, V," said Prince Seff, clapping again. "Despite your cupcakitosis, you've proven incredibly bright, so it's no surprise to me that you've figured all this out. What *is* a surprise to me, is why you've chosen such a dim-witted nut-ball to be your assistant."

"Don't call Instructor Verin a dim-witted nut-ball!" she retorted, her cheeks flushing with indignation. "He might be a little... *eccentric*, but I would bet my life on him over you, and anyone else in this galaxy, any day!"

"Is that so?" Prince Seff walked over to her and crouched down, but his focus was on the uneaten onion in his hand. "Then why isn't he here trying to save you?" A low chuckle rumbled through his chest. "Oh, I know—it's because he's running around somewhere, screaming and flapping his arms around like a helpless fledgling that's just fallen from a tree."

"I'm not, actually. I'm right here."

Heart suddenly beating faster, V looked over the prince's

shoulder. It was Instructor Verin! Shuffling towards them, he held a comb in one hand. In his other hand, was a faded, blue book. On his head, a bucket, pushed back just far enough to show his face. Dark circles under the eyes, tufts of ratty hair, a demeanor distinctly lacking in glamour… he was definitely not himself.

"Well, well, well…" Prince Seff stood up, "…the dim-witted nut-ball in the flesh."

At the same time, V heard some rustling and grunting behind her. Turning her head to the side, she saw Laquat army-crawling towards the pole she and the others were tied to. The old lady waved and pointed to the false teeth inside her mouth. Not wanting to draw attention to her, V quickly refocused on Prince Seff and Instructor Verin.

"You don't look too good, do you?" Prince Seff was saying. "Tell me, dim-witted nut-ball, why are you here?"

"To tickle you." Instructor Verin ran a comb down the side of his bucket. "You are a very bad squid and I'm not going to radiator my friend's pitchfork."

"What?" Prince Seff's forehead wrinkled.

"Sorry," said Instructor Verin. "My mind is still a bit giraffe, but I will do my pillow to explain: I know who you mango and what you've been shambling. It all elephant bubbled a year ago when a new shoe came into existence—Threka. A total BBQ when it came to applesauce, what with the pet-mess vacuum and all."

"A hot seller to be sure," said Prince Seff, still looking puzzled.

"Yes," agreed Instructor Verin. "And you would piglet, being the inventor."

Elba, Stuarp, Truj, and Bon gasped again.

"You invented the pet-mess vacuum?" said Stuarp. "I've been trying to get one of those for months!"

"They're all sold out," said the prince.

"Probably because they poodle quite well," Instructor Verin said to Stuarp. "But now, if you'll allow me to cheese my tusks."

"Of course," Stuarp said, apologetically. "Please, go on."

The instructor returned his attention to Prince Seff. "Now, as I was catapulting, you created the pet-mess vacuum, only you did it under the rug of that whale I saw on the swimming-pool a few weeks ago—the one that hair-dresses Threka."

"Are you talking about the bot that runs Threka?" V interjected.

"Yes. Isn't that what I gobbled?"

"No, but it's okay. I'll interpret." She turned to the others. "He meant to say that Prince Seff started Threka and created the pet-mess vacuum under the guise of a robot—the one everyone thinks owns the company. There was a picture of it on the news a few days ago."

"Hey! I saw that picture!" declared Elba. "The bot was standing beside the cardboard box Threka was started in!"

"Yes," said Prince Seff. "My father wouldn't let me work in the palace, so I had to use whatever I could find." He retrained his eyes on Instructor Verin. "As for *you*, those are hefty accusations, and you have no proof."

"Not yet, but it won't be macaroni before we find vittles that you're the grape of Threka, which is just a front company to both build and financially nebula the Planet Destroyer."

Prince Seff's dark eyes flashed. "Is that so?"

"Yes. By your own toothpaste, you are very good with computers and bots, so I have no reservations about casseroling you of this: you are the who, Threka is the where, but we still don't have the *clipboard*." Instructor Verin held up the faded, blue book. "I believe it's somewhere in here, but I can't understand a single fish-bowl of your language. In fact, the only thing I've been able to thunderstorm is that zaret means *heart*."

"Heart?" V racked her brain, but all she could think of was Itha's heart, the story Headmaster Baz had shouted to her while on his pain meds. According to legend, the heart was buried in the core of the first world Itha made, and was endowed with great powers of both peace and wisdom… "I know what it is!" she suddenly exclaimed. "The why! I just figured it out! The why *is* the *zaret*! That's what you've been searching for, isn't it, Prince Seff? That's why you got Headmaster Baz to help: you knew he'd do anything to find it! And you've been paying him with money from Threka!"

Before Prince Seff could answer, Instructor Verin took over. "Itha's Heart—I know that tennis ball! When it's not knuckled in Rohemish, that is!" He turned to the prince. "The waffle was a direct result of the dishwashers on Rohema, wasn't it? You were so tree-branch for puddles that you hiccupped for the pineapple, in ruffles that it would bring your nostril help, but in the bathtub, you had to echo other nostrils because the seatbelt said was taped in a planet's thumbnail!"

Prince Seff stared blankly at the instructor.

Stuarp politely cleared his throat. "Can you repeat that, please?"

Instructor Verin began again, but V cut him off after the part about teddy bears eating shoelaces.

"I think he meant to say that the Planet Destroyer is a direct result of the turmoil on Rohema, and that Prince Seff was so desperate for peace that he searched for the heart in hopes that it would help his people, but in the process, he had to destroy several ancient planets because, according to legend, the heart was in buried the core of Itha's first world." V paused to take a breath and then added, "Itha is said to have been the first worldmaker."

"Oh," Stuarp nodded. "That makes more sense."

"Perhaps I was wrong about you being a dim-witted nutball," Prince Seff said to Instructor Verin. "I must say, you are right on all counts, but just like the others, you will have to die. That's what happens to anyone who finds out the truth... no matter how much I happen to like them."

Something in his eyes startled V. "Autia..." she murmured. "You didn't hate her, you *cared* about her, but she found out what you were doing, so you had her planet blown up."

"Yes, it's true," Prince Seff admitted. "She wasn't my fiancé, but I did love her. As for her people, they were a bunch of savages who got what they deserved." His dark eyes flickered to Kesh. "Throw them in the frosting."

Kesh didn't move.

"Well, what are you waiting for?" the prince snapped. "You're just as guilty as I am."

For a few seconds, Kesh did nothing. But then, he suddenly launched himself at Prince Seff, knocking the uneaten onion out of his hand before seizing the onion pouch and throwing it into the frosting.

"You fool!" the prince roared. "Look at what you've done!"

"I'm tired of following your orders!" Kesh bellowed. "I'm older, so *I* should make the rules!"

"But I'm a *prince!*" Prince Seff sneered, tearing off one of Kesh's ears.

Howling with rage, Kesh yanked the prince's nose off and then tackled him to the ground.

Meanwhile, Laquat had finally reached the tied-up competitors. Plucking the false teeth from her mouth, she used them to untie Truj, and then Elba, who threw herself into the Rohems' bloody fray.

Also meanwhile, Instructor Verin hurried over to V. "We don't have much noodles," he said, attempting to untie her. But, his fingers kept fumbling with the knots, and it wasn't until Laquat lent him her false teeth that he was able to undo them.

"You knew all along it was Prince Seff, didn't you?" said V, pride swelling inside her chest; yes, the instructor was a bit of a dunce-head, but she was certain he was the most brilliant dunce-head in the whole galaxy.

"Not all toothbrush, but I did gargle my suspicions." He smiled a shaky, half-smile before scurrying over to Elba, and with Stuarp's help, pried her arms from Kesh's neck and her legs from Prince Seff's arm. No sooner had they gotten her free than the prince was overcome by a fit of giggles.

Everyone stopped and stared.

"What's going on?" Elba asked.

"It's the onions," panted Kesh. "When he doesn't eat enough of them, he giggles like a girl."

"So, what do we do?" V looked at Instructor Verin.

"Carriage them up and archive the PPC to let them cabbage they've got the wrong hot air balloon," he replied.

"Tie up the Rohems," V quickly explained to the others. "And we need to let the PPC know they've got the wrong man."

Tying up the prince was easy because he was giggling so hard that he didn't resist, nor did he resist V reclaiming her spatula. Kesh was a little harder, but with everyone helping, they got the job done.

"I'm sorry I wasn't a better husband, V!" he called out.

But V wasn't listening; she and the others were running up the stairs and had almost reached the top when Headmaster Baz appeared in the doorway. His eyes widened when he saw the competitors and Bon. They widened even more when he looked down and saw the Rohems, bloodied and subdued, the prince giggling like crazy.

"What in the name of all things decrepit is wrong with Prince Seff?" he asked.

"No more onions," said Truj.

"And he got his nose torn off," Elba added.

"Oh?" Headmaster Baz raised an eyebrow. "I don't care about his nose, but I have been wondering what would happen if he didn't eat those decrepit onions." A wicked grin flashed across his lips. "I suppose this all works out perfectly—with that decrepit prince and his decrepit bodyguard out of the way, I can have the money *and* the zaret. I can also be rid of all of you. Especially you, V—it would be impossible to count the number of aneurysms you've nearly given me. And you, Xander Verin, with your constant primping and perfect hair..." Visibly agitated, he ran a hand over his scarred head. "Well, I suppose I should go, seeing as only moments ago I summoned the Planet Destroyer to this decrepit planet!" Grinning again, he snapped his fingers and ran away.

34

A fierce gust of wind smacked V in the face and suddenly, she was careening through the air. Only, she wasn't falling, she was inside a typhoon, being whipped around the basement. Every once in a while, a pair of arms or legs streaked past her. She also saw a flash of purple hair, a white smudge that might have been a cat, and a fuzzy cloud. Opening her mouth, she tried to scream but nothing came out. Or maybe something did, she just couldn't hear it over the howling air and pelting drops of rain. The thought crossed her mind then, that Secretary Ophelia must have felt very similarly being trapped inside her tiny office with a tornado, but before she had time to really process that thought, the wind and rain suddenly stopped and she was falling—but only for a second, jolting to a halt midair. Heart racing and dripping wet, she quickly glanced around. Laquat, Truj, Giblit, Elba, Bon, Stuarp, Prince Seff, and Kesh were hovering beside her, and standing on the basement floor right below all of them, was Instructor Verin. No longer wearing his bucket—it likely having blown off in the typhoon—his arms were outstretched, and he wore a look of great concentration on his face.

Abruptly, V started moving again, but not in the same wild way she'd been whipping around before. This was a very slow, very controlled movement towards the center of the basement. A few times the air beneath her wavered, and each time she looked at the instructor. The strain on his face was visible; stopping a typhoon and saving everyone in the room from plummeting to their deaths was definitely hard work.

And then, she was falling again, landing with a splat on something soft and gooey. "Frosting!" she sputtered, spitting the sweet, white topping from her mouth. "Instructor Verin! Help! I'm in the vat of frosting!"

Within seconds, he was pulling her out. "I'm sorry," he panted. "This was the safest place to hat you—that typhoon really lunched it out of me."

"It's okay," she croaked. "Thank you for saving me." As she toppled to the floor, Instructor Verin rushed to help the others out of the frosting. Truj and Elba, who were staying afloat by repeatedly rolling from their stomachs to their backs, were too busy stuffing their faces and didn't want to get out.

"Fine," Laquat said. "I suppose you two can stay and wait for the Planet Destroyer, but *I'm* getting out of here." She hobbled to the stairs, globs of frosting dripping from her soaked purple hair and clothes.

"The Planet Destroyer!" Bon cried. The bandage on his head had blown off and his sparse scraggles of hair were sticking up every which way. "I completely forgot!" Slapping a frosting coated hand on his forehead he teetered to the side and fainted.

Aside from V, no one else noticed—they were too busy running around the basement, screaming. Even Kesh was screaming, but not Prince Seff—the only things coming from his mouth were giggles.

"This isn't helping!" V yelled, grabbing Instructor Verin's arm as he ran past. "We've got to get out of here!"

"You're right!" Coming to a halt, he cleared his throat and

shouted, "Everyone stop and cock-a-doodle-doo!"

The screaming and running abruptly stopped and several 'cock-a-doodle-doos!' echoed through the basement.

"He meant *run*!" V exclaimed.

Instructor Verin nodded and added, "Courtyard!"

A brief pause followed before Elba and Truj sprinted after Laquat. Stuarp, after grabbing Giblit and helping Bon to his feet, was right behind them. Instructor Verin and V followed, but halfway up the stairs, V stopped.

"Wait! What about them?" She looked at the Rohems. "Are we going to leave them here to die?"

"Well, yeah. They were pinecone to shower us," said Instructor Verin.

V's eyes went to Kesh. She wasn't by any means condoning what he'd done, but if not for him, she and the others would currently be drowning in frosting. "Kesh wasn't going to kill us."

Instructor Verin opened his mouth and closed it before dashing down to Kesh and untying him. "What he does now is up to sandwich," he said, dashing back to V and grasping her hand.

"I can live with that," she said.

The two of them sprinted up the remaining stairs, through the Blue Sparkle, and out into the courtyard where Bon, Giblit, and the other competitors were huddled together.

Whimpering, Truj pointed to the sky. Encroaching on the horizon was a black, crescent-shaped ship: the Planet Destroyer!

Elba burst into tears. "I'm not ready to die!" she wailed. "I still haven't swum through molten lava and lived!"

Bon was next to start crying. He was followed by Stuarp,

and then Truj. Laquat seemed to be the only one oblivious to what was going on, taking her false teeth from her mouth and wiping them down with her shirt.

"Sure, wish I could find my diamond teeth," she muttered.

Hearing a few sniffles beside her, V looked up and saw Instructor Verin wipe a tear from his cheek, his tired eyes meeting hers.

"I'm cookies about the other day," he said. "I parmesan have told you about Palfrey right from the pepperoni. I disappointed you and hurt your intestines, and I'm sorry." His lips wobbled into a smile. "You're the best-fuzzy I've ever had, even better than Palfrey when we were still fuzzies." He wiped another tear from his cheek.

Best fuzzy? V was stunned—did he really just call her his friend? Not only that, but his *best* friend? "No!"

"You don't sparkle to be my best-fuzzy?" Instructor Verin said, both looking and sounding hurt.

"No, I mean, *yes*, I *do* want to be your best-friend—I was saying 'no' to this situation; I didn't come all this way and make all that ridiculous not-real food and put up with all the craziness here just to *die!*

His eyes widened and his lips formed another smile, one that didn't wobble. "You're right!" he said. "There has to be snuffles we fork do!" His brow furrowed. "But turtle?"

Biting the inside of her cheek, V looked at the ship again. While everything she'd said was true—she really hadn't come all this way to die—how was she, or anyone else, supposed to stop a ship that was made for the sole purpose of blowing up planets? "I know!" she said a moment later. "*You* can stop it!"

"Me?" His eyes widened again.

"Yes! Try to make it into something!"

"Try to snuggle it into burritos?"

"Yes!" She pointed up. "Hurry!" A laser beam had materialized from the ship and was headed directly for them. "Instructor Verin, there's no time to waste!"

Jaw clenching, and throwing both arms into the air, his eyes locked onto the beam.

Seconds later, something splattered onto V's face: *mush*! It was raining from the sky, and then *pouring* from the sky, swirling around her, forming an ocean of thick, gloopy liquid!

She wrapped an arm around Instructor Verin's waist to keep him afloat. As she did so, Palfrey's hover-bus nosedived off the roof of the Blue Sparkle and landed in the mush. When the splatter died down, she saw Headmaster Baz on top of the hover-bus with Kesh. The Rohem was mercilessly tugging on the headmaster's ears and nose. In response, the headmaster pulled out a stun-gun, blasting Kesh with it before aiming it at Instructor Verin.

Attempting to stop him, V threw her spatula, but it fell short, hitting Prince Seff in the head as he swam around, giggling. Headmaster Baz laughed and re-aimed the stun-gun, but at that very moment, a silver spaceship swooped down from the sky and a bouquet of roses jumped out of it, onto the headmaster's back.

"Secretary Oph—!" V was cut short as a wave of mush crashed over her and the instructor, forcing them into the depths of the mushy ocean. Using all her strength, she kicked to the surface, but her body was quickly giving way to the stress it was under. She felt Instructor Verin fading too, his muscles weakening with every passing second. I can't do this, she thought, struggling to keep herself and him afloat. I can't do this...

It was then that a single word entered her mind: alone.

She'd always been alone. No one had ever cared about her—that was just normal life at the school. Only, she wasn't there any more... Her eyes flickered to Stuarp, Bon, Elba, Laquat, and Truj. You're not alone! She realized. You *can* do this—you just can't do it *alone*!

Spitting mush from her mouth, she yelled as loud as she could, "Elba, the Most Daring Girl Ever! Laquat, the Jewel Bedazzled Elder! Truj, the Wielder of the Ray-gun! Stuarp, the Cloud of Peace! Bon! I need your help!"

Within seconds, Elba swirled over in a fast-moving current, taking hold of one of the instructor's arms. Truj rolled across the top of the mush and took hold of the instructor's other arm. Looking very cloud-like, Stuarp bobbed over, grasping the other side of the instructor's waist. Bon, with Giblit clinging to the top of his head, dog-paddled over and pushed the instructor's mushy hair out of his face. Laquat rowed over on an outhouse door, leveling the edge of it right beneath the instructor's chin.

Together, with all six of them supporting Instructor Verin, it wasn't long before the Planet Destroyer exploded into a brilliant firework of mush.

35

After a rough couple of days, Instructor Verin's speech and appearance were back to normal; no more 'quacks' or 'pickles' intertwined in sentences, no more ratty tufts of hair or dark-circled eyes. There was also no more bucket, as it was lost in the typhoon, but he seemed fine without it, having finally realized that Stuarp, although a Kloud with a capitol K, was completely harmless.

"You ready, Vivi?" he asked.

"Yeah, I think so." V was glad it was dark so he couldn't see the silly grin on her face that just wouldn't come off; ever since the mush-storm ended and he'd cleaned up the mess with nothing more than a snap of his fingers, it had been inked to her face like a dark-pink tattoo.

"Okay, then, here we go." He took her hand and together, they stepped out of the closet and into the lobby of the Blue Sparkle, which was bursting with flashing lights. Not far from them, Secretary Ophelia was arrayed in bundles of sparkly-blue flowers and a matching t-shirt that read, '#PPCSAVESLIVES'. "Good thing she showed up when she did," Instructor Verin said, nodding to the secretary.

"Right?" V silently applauded herself for writing her plea for help into the next 'Perpetually Unending Story' article. It was probably a little confusing to readers when Lagatha cried for Ophelia, the Magnificent Mute, to help her as Instructor

Handsome fell into the hands of Lord Raff. But, it had worked—the secretary came, saving both her's and Instructor Verin's lives, as well as the entire planet of Fooda.

"Secretary Ophelia," a reporter said. "Is it true that you're contemplating joining the Galactic Wrestling Team?"

Secretary Ophelia stared at the reporter, a smirk on her face.

"Secretary Ophelia," tried a second reporter. "Are you making a statement by never speaking? Perhaps you feel there are too many people in this galaxy who are constantly speaking, and are therefore making a protest for silence?"

Again, she said nothing, but the reporters continued their questioning, seemingly determined to get her to say *something* about *anything*.

On the other side of the lobby, Bon, Giblit, Elba, Laquat, Stuarp, and Truj were surrounded by another group of reporters. Bon and Elba were smiling and seemed happy with the attention; Giblit was perched on Bon's shoulder, cleaning his tail; Stuarp was bowing repeatedly; Laquat was showing one of the reporters her false teeth while giving a detailed description of her stolen diamond teeth; and Truj was swirling both hands through the air as though painting with invisible paint.

"How does it feel knowing you helped save a planet?" a reporter called out to Elba.

"Great!" she replied. "I fully intend to continue on in this profession."

"Profession? Can you expound?"

"Yes—I fully intend to continue on in the profession of saving planets from epic destruction."

"How are you going to do that now that the Planet

Destroyer is gone?"

"I don't know." Elba blew a bubble and sucked it back into her mouth. "I'm sure I'll think of something."

"What about you, Truj?" another reporter asked. "Fans of the Baking Adventures H-I-J-K-L-M-N-O-P Competition have been very intrigued with your acrobatic skills and love of creating art. How do you feel those two things have influenced your ability to help save Fooda?"

Truj's arms stopped swirling. "Uh..." He or she reached into his or her pocket and pulled out a smashed cupcake, taking a bite of it before smearing it on the reporter's camera..

Meanwhile, a group of female reporters had gathered around Instructor Verin.

"Tell us about your daring plan to save Fooda," one of them said, batting her abnormally long eyelashes. "Is it true that you figured out Prince Seff was using the billions of pet-mess vacuum commercials played daily to conceal the signals of the Planet Destroyer?"

"Possibly," he said. "We're still looking into..."

Another reporter bumped the eyelash reporter aside with her wide, curvy hips. "Have you always been so talented at making mush out of laser beams and planet-destroying ships?" she asked.

A third reporter stomped her stiletto heel on the foot of the curvy-hipped reporter. Ignoring the shrill howls of pain, she smiled and puckered her unusually full lips. "Whatever happened to your girlfriend?"

"Well—" he began.

"Hey!" someone shouted. "Mr. Dolop's finally here!"

In a matter of seconds, Instructor Verin was forgotten and every camera and flashing light in the lobby changed direction, homing in on the worldmaker as he strode through the open front doors of the Blue Sparkle.

"Mr. Dolop! Now that you've been released, can you tell us how you feel about being framed for such an unspeakably, heinous crime?" a reporter asked.

"Shocked and hurt," said Palfrey.

"What about those responsible? Did you suspect Prince Seff from the beginning?"

Palfrey shook his head of perfectly combed hair and slipped both hands into his well-pressed trouser pockets. "No, I did not. I only knew that someone was heartlessly destroying our galaxy one planet at a time, and that I was going to do everything I could to bring them to justice."

"When did you first suspect the prince?" someone else asked.

"On the first day of the competition when I found pieces of raw onion strewn across the floor of my penthouse. But that wasn't grounds to suspect him of anything other than breaking and entering—until I saw that my scrapbook had been moved. That got me wondering if he somehow knew I was tracking the Planet Destroyer; little did I know he'd use my own work against me, even using it to frame me for *his* crimes."

"Do you feel that Prince Seff Pip's, Kesh Yib's, and that crazy headmaster's punishments are justice enough?" a different reporter asked.

"I do. There are worse things than death and slumming through sewage to extract toilet paper for recycling is one of those things."

"Speaking of sewage and recycling toilet paper, how do you feel about the allegations that cupcake wrappers on Fooda are made from recycled toilet paper?"

"Fine, although, no one was supposed to know about that, but now that everyone seems to, it's important to understand that all the toilet paper is chemically treated and burned before reconstitution into said product. I mean, you eat food that's grown in fertilizer, don't you? And you do know what fertilizer is, right? So, what's the problem?"

A hush fell over the lobby and intermittent sounds of gagging were heard.

"So," another reporter asked, "What do you intend to do now? Is it accurate to say you've spent all your money and sold many of your resources trying to find the Planet Destroyer? Even having gone so far as to continue airing the Baking Adventures Fraggle-Daggle-Baggle-Rocky-Roo Competition after two deaths took place on set?"

A look of annoyance crossed Palfrey's face. "It's the *Baking Adventures Fun-Times-For-Everyone-All-The-Time Competition,*" he said, emphasizing each word. "And yes, that is accurate. Many people do not know this, but Ton, the first planet destroyed, was my home world. Thus, I took its destruction very personally and swore justice would be done. That is the sole reason I started the show—the name of which you can't seem to ever get right—to fund that mission. And I felt no shame in using it as such, even after tragedy struck—it was all for a bigger cause. But now that it's over, I'm completely worn out. Therefore, I've decided to retire to Greena, my first-made world. There, I shall live a quiet, peaceful life until I decide to resume worldmaking."

Several questions came at once.

"It's been a really long past few days," Palfrey said, shouting to be heard. "So, I'm sure you will all understand when I ask you to please leave the Blue Sparkle and *go home.*"

But the questions only increased.

Annoyance crossing his face again, Palfrey raised a hand in the air and flicked a few fingers. Moments later, a bot with a firehose tromped into the lobby, spraying everyone inside. Arms flailed, toes were trampled, screams turned into water-logged gurgles, and cameras clattered to the floor. When the water shut off, the drenched reporters sloshed out of the building.

Hooting and hollering, Elba, Stuarp, Truj, and Laquat began slipping and sliding on the floor. Bon and Giblit went to get the camcorder, V wrung out her hair, and Instructor Verin pulled out his comb.

"Xander Verin!" Palfrey called out. Soaked, but smiling, he walked up to the instructor and extended a hand. "I haven't had a chance to thank you for what you did. I'm so grateful and will forever be in your debt."

V, now wringing out the skirt of her dress, watched Instructor Verin hesitate; would he be able to let go of the cruel, heartless Palfrey he'd once known and make way for the humbled, grateful Palfrey that was standing before him? The seconds slowly ticked by and she started to worry, but then a wide smile lit up his face.

"You're welcome," he said, taking Palfrey's hand and shaking it. "It was an honor to help."

"Quite a trick there, making mush," said Palfrey. "There's only one other person I've met that could do that."

"And all this time I thought I was the only one," said Instructor Verin with a chuckle.

"Yes, well, it seems that you're not," said Palfrey, a bemused expression on his face. "Thank you, again." His eyes flickered to V. "Xander, would you give this lovely lady and me a moment alone, please?"

"Of course." Instructor Verin winked at V before stepping away.

Turning to her, Palfrey clasped one of her hands in his. "I want to thank you for the part you played in all this."

V's lips turned down. "You shouldn't be thanking me, Palfrey. It's because I found your chart of destroyed planets that you were arrested and sent to prison."

"True. But how were you supposed to know that Prince Seff and Kesh snuck into my penthouse through a ceiling vent and added Oruka? If you hadn't found the chart they would have made sure someone else had, and chances are that person wouldn't have figured out what was really going on."

"But that's just it—I knew something was wrong and instead of bringing it up to you, I acted like a child tattling on a friend."

"No, you did what any normal person would have done, what *I* would have done. Approaching someone with damning evidence of destroying planets isn't exactly a smart thing to do."

"I guess you're right," said V.

"I *am* right," Palfrey replied. "So stop feeling like you've ruined my life because in all reality, you *saved* it.

Despite his graciousness, V still felt awful. "Well, it wasn't just me. It was mostly Instructor Verin. And Bon, Stuarp, Laquat, Elba, and Truj—they helped too."

"I know, and I'm grateful to them as well. However, if you hadn't inspired them to do what they did, Fooda would be gone and I'd be rotting in a cell—so, thank you." Palfrey lifted V's hand to his lips and lightly kissed it behind the knuckles. "Will you come to Greena with me? Regardless of what most people think, my life is quite dull and lonely."

Caught off guard, V's cheeks turned bright red and she glanced away. "I... well... I..." That's when she saw Ursa Dazzle-Razzle, who'd somehow slipped into the lobby unnoticed, wrapped in Instructor Verin's arms. Choking on a breath, she looked back at Palfrey. But he was no longer looking at her. *He too,* was looking at Ursa.

"Excuse me, will you?" he said. Without waiting for an answer, he let go of her hand and hurried towards the red head.

The muscles in V's chest tightened and her stomach sank. Suddenly feeling all alone, her eyes swept the lobby. Briefly, she considered joining Elba and the others, but they were so happy. And right then, she *wasn't* happy. All trace of her dark-pink, tattooed smile gone, she trudged up to the roof where Palfrey's hover-bus was docked.

"Take me back to the Deluxe Worldmaker School For Worldmakers, please," she said to the bot stationed beside it.

"As you wish." The bot turned and tromped onto the hover-bus.

V was right behind it.

36

Arms full of rags, buckets, mops, and brooms, V waded into the flooded kitchen. Grula was at the stove making biscuits, and Headmaster Jiji—as he insisted on being called—had stopped by for a cupcake, which he was eating on his step stool. Ignoring his pitiful attempts at flattery, and the cook's spiteful looks, V headed straight for the cleaning closet. On the telly, a news report had just begun. In it, Instructor Verin and a gladiola-festooned Secretary Ophelia were standing in front of the PPC Headquarters. V bit her lip and silently told herself that she didn't want to see the report, that she had better things to do. And yet, she couldn't help stopping to watch,

"Mr. Verin," said a reporter, "now that the whole galaxy knows you're actually a spy, can you tell us when you first suspected Prince Seff Pip's involvement in the recent atrocities that have haunted our galaxy?"

"Of course," said Instructor Verin. "It was the evening before the show started when Prince Seff somehow knew everything about cupcakitosis, which, in and of itself, doesn't seem very suspicious, but considering how I only told Palfrey Dolop and Headmaster Baz what the disease really was, it was very strange. And as suspicions were already raised by V that the prince and headmaster were in some way connected, it was my first clue that they were up to something. Only, I didn't know what until Rainbow Jon was found dead."

"What was it about Rainbow Jon's death that led to this realization?" asked the reporter.

"Well, while we were at the Blue Sparkle, V overheard a conversation involving two people speaking about someone taking a bite of something to make them happy. At the time, neither one of us knew what it meant, but when Rainbow Jon died, it suddenly made sense: he was the one making all the cakes, cupcakes, and pancakes, which meant he was the one who'd put poison into Ha's cake. Only, he had no idea what he was doing; in the private interview I just had with Prince Seff, he admitted to giving Rainbow Jon the poison under the pretense that it was a 'happy' tonic. And having experienced firsthand Ha's gruff demeanor and hot-temper, there's no question in my mind why Rainbow Jon did what he did—he thought he was helping."

"And Rainbow Jon's death was Prince Seff's way of getting rid of evidence, so to speak?"

"Yes," said Instructor Verin.

"But why would Prince Seff want to poison Ha? They'd never met prior to the show."

"True, but it was never about Ha, it was always about framing Palfrey Dolop."

The reporter cocked his head to the side. "Can you explain in a little more detail, please?"

"Certainly. Prince Seff knew Palfrey was on to him and rather than let himself get caught, decided to make it look like Palfrey was the one responsible for the Planet Destroyer—which was why he went onto the show. But when he got there, he realized a diversion was needed to give him time to plant evidence."

"Which is why he killed Ha?"

"Yes."

"But why Ha? Why not someone else?"

"Because Ha was the easiest target. When we were at the briefing for the show, Ha made a statement about loving lemon-strawberry cake. And when he died, it was because of poison in the lemon-strawberry cake he'd just eaten. All Prince Seff had to do was program the bot to give certain cakes to certain people, and when the bot gave the prince the lemon-strawberry cake—he purposefully did this to deflect suspicion away from himself—he knew it was only a matter of time before Ha noticed and snatched it away."

"Prince Seff told us the cake was in the trash when Ha took it. Could that be used as an argument to prove he's actually innocent?"

"No." Instructor Verin shook his head. "V just happened to see some parchment paper poking out of the cake and knowing it might be made from recycled toilet paper, took it and—."

The telly turned off and Jiji cleared his throat. "That was enough of that." Turning to V, he suddenly knelt down on his step stool. Just as suddenly, Grula threw her pan of biscuits at his face, knocking him off the stool and into the flood.

"You're job isn't to stand around eating cupcakes and making proposals!" she barked. "If you insist on making me do all this work by myself, then at least do the job you're *supposed* to be doing!" She picked up an empty pot and threw it at him too, before splashing out of the kitchen.

V didn't care for Jiji's ridiculous behavior either, but couldn't leave him lying in the water, blubbering like a baby. Letting out a huff of air, she dropped her armful of cleaning supplies and went to help him when the lights flickered out. Letting out another huff of air, she left him to fend for himself and felt her way into the basement where she flipped the breakers, turning the lights back on.

Splash-clunk. Splash-clunk.

"Ah, Vivi, I'm so glad it's you. This would've been rather awkward had you been Jiji or Grula."

V froze, realizing then that the lights hadn't gone out on their own. "Instructor Verin?" Heart beating a little faster, she slowly turned around and saw him standing a few feet away. Above each of his shins, the top of a bucket could be seen poking out of the water. "What are you doing here? I just saw you on the news, at the PPC Headquarters."

"Yes, well, as we both know, spaceships travel quite speedily these days."

"Right, um…. shouldn't you be off somewhere with Ursa?"

"No. You were right about her."

"I was right about her?"

"Yes, remember when you said she didn't suit me? Well, you were right—not only is she not very nice, but she's also been imprisoned for embezzling money from a planet murderer. Apparently, she was using the money to pay for her numerous spa treatments."

"Oh." V paused to collect her thoughts, a strange feeling wriggling free inside her. "So…are you saying you *broke-up* with her?"

"Yes. Only, I didn't know about her criminal activities when I told her I no longer wanted to see her. Speaking of which, what happened at the Blue Sparkle? One moment you were there, and the next you were gone."

"Oh, um…" V scrambled for an explanation; she could hardly say that her reason for leaving was distress over his reunion with Ursa. "I guess I was just tired and decided to come back."

"Even after Palfrey asked you to go to Greena with him?"

Cheeks turning pink, she replied, "You know about that?"

"Yes. If I understood correctly, Palfrey told Bon who told Stuarp who told Laquat who then told me. Although, it did take some deciphering to fully make sense of it amidst all the talk of stolen jewels."

"Yeah, well, Palfrey seems to have a thing for Ursa—he beelined it over to her the moment he noticed she was there."

"Vivi, Ursa is his *mom*."

"*She is?*"

Instructor Verin nodded. "I was surprised too, believe me. What gave it away was Ursa pulling out a handkerchief, spitting on it, and then using it to clean Palfrey's face. The man squirmed like a worm trying to get away." He chuckled. "But enough about Ursa and Palfrey, I didn't come here to talk about them, I came here to tell you that you're no longer property of the school—you can leave any time you want."

A lump rose in V's throat and for a moment, she couldn't breathe. It didn't help that the strange feeling was growing stronger.

"Vivi, are you okay?" Instructor Verin splash-clunked a step closer and set a hand on her shoulder.

V tried to nod but couldn't. She should have been elated, bursting with joy, but she wasn't. It occurred to her then, that her whole life she'd only ever wanted two things: to leave the school and to write an ending for the 'Perpetually Unending Story' articles. And yet, while both of those things were worthy aspirations, she now knew they alone would never make her happy. What *would* make her happy, and what she'd recently *found* to make her happy, were kindness and friendship. Looking up into Instructor Verin's eyes, a rush of words spilled from her mouth, "I threw your book of 'Perpetually Unending Story' articles out the window of the Blue Sparkle. I'm so sorry! I just was worried you'd figure out I was the one writing them."

"I know," he said.

"You do?"

"Yes, I know about both of those things. What I don't know is why you didn't just tell me."

"I…" She sucked in a shallow breath of air; the strange feeling was everywhere now. "I was embarrassed that I could never finish it. It just kept going on and on and on because every time I *did* try to finish it, I died."

Instructor Verin's forehead wrinkled. "*You* died?"

"Yeah, I always envisioned myself as the main character."

"Lagatha, the Sock-Mender?"

"Yeah, but you should know that I was recently able to solve my problem and finish the story."

"Oh? How so?"

"Turns out, all I needed was some help from a few friends."

A smile tugging at his lips, Instructor Verin replied, "And those friends wouldn't happen to be a bunch of wackadoodles, would they? Say, from a baking show we may have recently been on?"

Nodding, V finally understood the strange feeling inside her: affection. And there was something else in there, too: gratitude—if not for the instructor, she never would have had the confidence, or necessity, to do what she'd done. "But the most help came from the wackadoodle that's standing in front of me." And with that, she threw her arms around Instructor Verin's neck.

37

It was the middle of the night and aside from a raccoon sniffing around on the countertops, the school's kitchen was empty. Stepping into a drawer, one of the raccoon's paws pressed the remote and the telly sputtered on,

"And now," a newswoman was saying. "We have an update on all of our favorite competitor-heroes from the most recent Baking Boopity-Bop-Hop-Funny-Competition Times. Only two weeks ago, they were inside the infamous rainbow teepee baking up a storm of unappetizing food and saving the galaxy, but where are they now?"

A picture popped up. It was of Laquat, Truj, Stuarp, Elba, V, and Instructor Verin, all of whom were smiling.

"Let's find out, shall we?"

The picture changed to a recording obscured by enormous amounts of steam. Suddenly, Elba's face appeared right in front of the camera,

"Hi everyone!" she said, pointing to something behind her. "This is where I'm practicing my lava-swim! It's not real lava, but in order to replicate its consistency, my mom and dad filled our indoor swimming pool with pudding and heated it. So far, I've only made it halfway across before almost drowning, but I'm working on it!" She smiled a wide, toothy smile. "Would you like to try swimming in it, Phill?" she asked the cameraman.

"No."

"Oh, come on. It'll be fun."

"No," said Phill. "I'm really okay."

Elba's smile flat-lined and her cheeks turned bright red. Letting out an ear-splitting shriek, she rushed at Phill, who took off running. Seconds later, Phill and the camera lurched forward into the pudding. A muffled scream and a few glub, glub, glubs sounded.

"Next time, you'll say yes!" Elba screeched. "Mom! Call the ambulance! The camera man is drowning!"

The recording ended and the newswoman returned to the telly, a smirk on her lips. "It's too bad Prince Seff wasn't there to hang Elba upside down by her toes!" A muted voice came from somewhere in the background and the smirk disappeared. Clearing her throat, the newswoman said, "What I meant was, I'm sure that's what Phil was thinking as he fell into the pool of pudding. Now, onto our next competitor: Laquat."

A video recording of Laquat hobbling around a tree started playing. Every so often, the purple-haired lady would stop and shake her cane up into the branches,

"Get down here, Grannie Upsha!" she demanded in a croaky voice. "Give back my ruby tooth right this instant!"

The camera zoomed in on the tree, revealing a hissing and spitting orange cat. The camera then retracted, focusing on Laquat as she resumed hobbling. After another turn around the tree, she shook her cane again and demanded that her "Grannie" give back her emerald tooth. This went on for a good fifteen minutes before the recording ended.

The next recording was of Truj. He or she was sleeping in a flower garden with a pink pansy between his or her teeth. A yellow bird swooped down and landed on his or her shoulder, hopped around a bit, and then flew away. That was the end of the recording.

Stuarp was next. Wearing his cloud costume, he was showing how different types of dancing could increase cloud formation.

A picture of V and Instructor Verin followed. In it, they were standing on the front steps of the school.

"Last, but not least," said the newswoman, "We have our final competitor, V. Unfortunately, we were unable to get an interview or recording of her so I will briefly update you on her doings." After putting on a pair of spectacles, the newswoman picked up a piece of paper and began reading from it. "Aside from being the author of the 'Perpetually Unending Story' articles, it seems that V and her best-fuzzy, Xander Verin, have purchased the Deluxe Worldmaker School For Worldmakers and have turned it into an 'I Can' school, where worldmakers who are down on their luck, or simply have no talent, can be taught new skills that focus on what they *can* do. Not on what they *can't* do. There was some backlash to this, though, from the former headmaster, Jiji."

The picture of V and Instructor Verin was replaced by a picture of Jiji. Standing on his step stool, he was in front of the school holding a picket sign that read, No! I'm the Headmaster!

"While Jiji's solitary efforts to stop this transition from happening didn't work, they did yield some beneficial results for him. As we recently learned, V was not really suffering from cupcakitosis, but, due to the heightened publicity of the disease, one very astute doctor saw Jiji on the telly and diagnosed *him* with the disease. Jiji is now being treated in a facility and is doing quite well."

A recording of Jiji began playing. He was on a white patio sitting in a white rocking chair. Tucked beneath one of his arms was his step stool, and in each of his hands was a cupcake. Serenely rocking back and forth, he would every so often take a bite of one cupcake and then the other. When the cupcakes were gone, a man in white scrubs brought him two more.

"Jiji's co-worker, Grula, is also doing quite well," read the newswoman, "and is working in the kitchen of the treatment facility where Jiji now lives. Currently, she's competing in an episode of the Baking Bippity-Bop-Hop-Adventures Competition."

A picture of Grula popped up. A potential smile on her ruddy, plump face, she was holding a tray of twelve cupcakes that had been decorated to look like squirrels. Printed on her apron were the words, 'Lagatha Was Really A Cupcake Maker'.

"As for the secretary of the worldmaker school, she, not really being a secretary at all, but a spy, has resumed work with the PPC."

A picture of Secretary Ophelia replaced the picture of Grula. Sporting a pair of daffodil bedecked glasses, she was inside a large office, sitting behind a desk. On the floor next to the desk, was a huge, stuffed hippopotamus.

"And that is all for our update on the competitor-heroes who recently saved the galaxy." The newswoman removed her spectacles and set down the piece of paper. "Now, on to our next story: Why billions of people have stopped eating fresh produce and are only eating foods created from manmade chemicals…"

The raccoon stepped on the remote again and the telly sputtered off.

38

Three months later…

"Hey, Vivi!" Instructor Verin called from the kitchen. "You gotta come see this!"

"Coming!" V grabbed a jar of beets and hurried out of the pantry.

"Up there," he said, pointing to the telly.

Looking up, V saw a preview playing for a new movie. "What…?" The blood drained from her face and she grabbed Instructor Verin's arm; when Stuarp had called to tell her that Bon's recording of their little adventure was being made into a movie, she thought he meant a *home* movie, not a *real* movie.

"Looks like Bon finally got his wish of becoming a film-maker. And guess who the star of his first film is?"

V's stomach clenched. "Me?"

"Yep." Instructor Verin took the jar of beats and floated it to the countertop. He then pried his arm out of V's hand and slipped it around her shoulders. "Don't sound so terrified; not only are you a galactically-renowned author, but you're about to become a galactically-renowned actress."

"Yeah… I'm not so sure that's something to be proud of…"

"Pish-posh—you'll be great. Besides, Bon dedicated the movie to Ha and Rainbow Jon."

V tried to smile, but just then, the preview for Bon's first ever movie ended, and the Saturday Night Hopefully Real and Sincere Criminal Confessions with Buford Buttlet came on,

"And now," said a man with purple hair. "We will resume our interview with the planet murderer, Prince Seff Pip of Rohema."

Icy chills ran down V's spine and she suddenly didn't care so much about her newly discovered career as an "actress". "Did he just say Prince Seff Pip?"

"He did, indeed," said Instructor Verin.

Seconds later, two stools floated over and they sat down, watching as a small grey room appeared on the telly. Inside of it, were two chairs. Seated on one of the chairs was an older man wearing glasses: Buford Buttlet. Seated on the other chair was Prince Seff.

"Tell us about this infamous *zaret*," Buford said.

Scowling, Prince Seff scratched a lumpy scar in the center of his face—the place where his nose had once been. "Turns out it was nothing more than a real-life mummified heart—no power at all. I think Itha knew he was going to die so he crawled into the core of Oruka; you always find what you're looking for in the last place you look, right?" He snickered, and then grew serious. "Yeah, he knew he was about to die so he tore his own heart out. The whole thing was a sham."

"How do you know he tore his own heart out?"

"Because his body was lying right next to it—Headmaster Baz had pictures."

"Right," said Buford, sounding doubtful. "And just to be clear, you thought this heart would somehow bring peace to your home world of Rohema?"

"Yes."

"So it must have been devastating when you learned that everyone on Rohema killed each other, leaving no survivors."

Prince Seff shrugged. "Not really. It actually made me feel good—they were all so violent and cruel towards one another. I'll consider it a job well done."

Visibly disturbed, Buford scooted his chair back a few feet. "Why don't you tell us what you do when you're not slumming through the sewers looking for toilet paper to recycle? You've gotten quite involved in some of the reformation programs here at the PPC Penitentiary, isn't that, right? Will you tell us a little about them?"

The brusque expression on the prince's face faded into a cheerful smile. "Absolutely! There's a sewing class taught by my bodyguard, Kesh Yib. He's been very successful at helping inmates recycle old bed sheets into things like porch swings and bicycles—one woman even managed to make a backhoe. It's quite amazing to see the amount of creativity this prison holds."

A picture popped up on the telly. It showed Kesh sitting at a table, hunched over a sewing machine and a white dress. Another picture popped up beside it showing a porch swing and bicycle, both made from bed sheets. The next picture to pop up was of the backhoe, only, it was made from metal.

"Yes, I'm sure it is," Buford said, adjusting his glasses. "What about the other classes?"

"Well, there's an archeology class taught by Headmaster Baz. Currently, he's working on teaching everyone how to excavate their prison cells for rare artifacts."

The sewing pictures were replaced by pictures of the headmaster. In the first one, he was standing beside a chalkboard, pointing to a drawing of a shovel. In the second one, he was standing inside his cell, shovel in hand, surrounded by enormous piles of dirt.

"How very—" Buford started to say.

"And Ursa," the prince cut-in, "she started an in-prison spa that uses residual dirt from the excavating for mud-baths." He brushed a hand over his arm. "Smooth as silk—you won't find anything better."

A picture of Ursa, standing beside an old bathtub filled with mud, appeared. Her brilliant red hair was fading to pink, and her youthful face was beginning to sag.

"I was under the impression that you hated Ursa," said Buford. "After all, she stole an enormous amount of money from your front-company, Threka."

"True," the prince admitted. "But it didn't take us long to bond over the fact that we both know Xander Verin—he's the one who put me in here *and* he broke Ursa's heart. With that under our belts, we were able to put the past in the past and move on with our new endeavors."

"I see. And what about you? You also teach a class, isn't that, right?"

"Yes—Pretend Food Baking. It was inspired by my experience in the Baking Adventures Fun-Times-For-Everyone-All-The-Time Competition."

Next was a picture of Prince Seff. He was standing beside a table strewn with rusty metal bars, old door-locks, yellowed-toilet seats, cracked mirrors, and broken sinks. In his hands was what looked like an ice-cream cone made from a piece of broken pipe and an old door knob.

"This is all very intriguing, but in the interest of time, we must be moving on," Buford said. "In memory of the beloved show, is there anything you would like to say to your former competitors before I leave?"

"There is, actually." Turning in his seat, Prince Seff stared right into the camera. "V, I just want you to know that I forgive you for helping that assistant of yours put me in here." He lifted a shiny, silver something and waved it.

"Hey!" said V. "That's my spatula!"

"You're probably wondering why I have your spatula," he went on. "I kept it as a memento of our friendship. Yes, I know, it's been a little rough with me trying to kill you and you throwing this piece of cookware at my head, but I still like to think that you and I are fond of one another. Which is why it makes me sad that you haven't been by to visit yet—it's very clean here, a lot nicer than that run-down school you decided to buy." He reached into his jumpsuit pocket and pulled out an onion, taking a bite. "Oh, and Kesh says 'hi' and wants you to know he's almost done sewing your wedding dress. Yes, he told me about your marriage, and considering everything that's happened, I finally decided to give him my blessing. So, just a heads up—when we break out of here, he plans on having a proper ceremony."

www.ingramcontent.com/pod-product-compliance
Lightning Source LLC
LaVergne TN
LVHW091536060526
838200LV00036B/631